deaf
not Deaf

by Christian Fusco

deaf not Deaf is a work of fiction. Inspired by the experiences of the author, characters, names, dates, places, events, and details have been changed for dramatic purposes or are entirely creations of the author's imagination. Certain characters may be composites and should not be considered true representations of anyone real.

ISBN 978-0-578-94823-2

For Mia and Roman-
Never be afraid to try, and never be afraid to fail.

Acknowledgements

A special thank you to Justina Miles and Kelly Corrigan for your friendship and for your creative input.

Thank you to my editor, Ellen Todras, my cover artist, Kostis Pavlou, and my mentor Dr. Diane Klein for all the help you provided me in making this novel a reality.

Thank you to all of you I consider my Hancock family.

Finally, thank you to my beautiful wife, Melissa, who no matter what I try, continues to believe in me.

Table of Contents

AUTHOR'S NOTE

I started writing *deaf not Deaf* in 2018, nineteen years into my career as a teacher of the Deaf and Hard of Hearing. The first decade of my career was spent working with Deaf and Hard of Hearing students in Chicago and in Philadelphia. The setting of the book, John Hancock Elementary School, is based on a real Philadelphia public school called John Hancock Demonstration School. I spent seven years teaching Deaf and Hard of Hearing children there. It is a school that will forever hold a special place in my heart.

You will notice in the title and throughout the story the word "deaf" is sometimes capitalized and other times it is not. Capital 'D' Deaf refers to a group of people that share a language, American Sign Language, as well as a common set of beliefs and practices. In other words, to be capital 'D' Deaf is to be part of a cultural group.

When the word is not capitalized, it refers to the condition of not being able to hear sound. People who are deaf typically have hearing parents and go to schools where spoken English is the only language used by teachers and staff.

Most deaf children are born into hearing families. Cochlear implants allow parents to speak to their child and to have that child hear their voice. That was not possible for most parents of deaf children twenty years ago. As amazing as cochlear implant technology is it represents a threat to the Deaf community.

It is estimated that fewer than 500,000 people use American Sign Language in the United States today. As more parents choose to have their deaf children implanted, the number of people who learn ASL and become members of the Deaf community gets smaller. This is why Deaf people object to cochlear implant technology.

This book was written to introduce hearing people to a world they may not know or understand. It explores the differences in deafness and the possibilities that exist when people put aside their bias and get to know a person's true character.

Words and phrases signed in the book can be found on www.deafnotDeaf.net. Video links on the website will show you how to properly express the signed dialogue in the story organized by chapter. There are also video clips that explore themes in the book, explanations of Deaf culture, and rules to remember when using sign language.

In addition, signs used by the characters Luis, Jennifer and Julio in the eBook version have a hyperlink embedded in the text that will take the reader to a video clip that demonstrate how these characters' words and phrases are expressed in sign language. All signs are performed by Justina Miles, a talented young Deaf woman who also is a former student of yours' truly!

Writing signed dialogue was a unique challenge to me as an author. There is no written form of American Sign Language. All of the dialogue signed in the book is hyphenated and italicized to distinguish it from the spoken dialogue. You will notice that sometimes individual words appear between hyphens and other times phrases are between the hyphens.

I wrote the signed dialogue this way because Deaf people do not use signs for pronouns, articles and forms of the verb *to be*. Those words are implied, or are communicated through facial expression, the use of space, and body language.

An example of this can be found in Chapter 4. Luis argues with his mother about joining a basketball league after school. Jennifer, his mother, wants to know who will bring him to practice.

I wrote one of her questions to him about it as, *Who-will bring-you?* The words *who, bring,* and *you* are all signed. However, the word *will* is not signed, it is implied. So the words *will bring* are placed together between hyphens to communicate the message clearly for the reader without suggesting the word *will* is actually signed by the Luis's mother.

2

American Sign Language is what attracted me to Deaf education over twenty five years ago and it has allowed me to make friendships with people I would have never know had I not learned it. I encourage everyone reading *deaf not Deaf* to take the time to learn to sign and make friends in the Deaf community.

1

RIAN RADIGAN

Rian stood by herself in the John Hancock Elementary schoolyard. Although the school year started two weeks earlier, today was her first day. She thought it was strange to call this a schoolyard. There were no swings, monkey bars, or ball fields. There wasn't even any grass. It was nothing more than a sprawling sea of asphalt keeping the circular, brick, elementary school building afloat.

A three-foot-high, green chain-link fence separated the Hancock students from Millbrook Road and the duplexes that made up the Millbrook Park community. A sorry little patch of trees, pretending to be a forest, sat neatly behind the fence opposite the strange round building. The fourth wall in this urban schoolyard consisted of a large hill, paved completely in brown brick. The brick jutted out and up from years of undergrowth pushing back against the clay facade. A steep set of concrete stairs ran up the hill leading to a drop-off spot for students.

That was the spot where Rian's mother, Joanna, dropped her off a few hours earlier. Rian did not want to come to John Hancock Elementary School. She didn't want to move to Millbrook Park for that matter, but as she was learning, some things were not within her control.

If it were up to her, her parents would still be married. The fighting would have stopped, and they would still love each other. They did love each other once, but that was a long time ago.

Now, Millbrook Park was her new reality. She no longer lived in a house with a big yard. She no longer lived in the same neighborhood as her best friend, Sarah. There was no tall maple tree in the front yard to climb or a basketball hoop in her driveway to practice free throws. There was no driveway at all. Her home was gone, her friends were far away, and her dad had a new life and a new girlfriend. Rian hated all of it.

"What are those things stuck to your head?" she heard a boys voice crack from behind her.

Rian was so busy feeling sorry for herself, she didn't notice two boys from her class approach her. The boy who spoke was Gerry Shack. She had spent the morning watching him harass another boy named Lucas. Shack, as he was called by the other sixth-grade students, tore the eraser from his pencil and pressed it into the back of Lucas's head.

For forty minutes during Reading, and another twenty minutes after that, this brute tormented poor Lucas, a much smaller student. Rian wondered why Lucas didn't say something. She watched him shift in his seat and try to change the position of his desk in order to avoid Shack's pencil, but basically he just accepted the abuse.

Shack's greasy, dark-brown hair was slathered in gel and parted to the right. He was tall and oafish and his hunched shoulders emphasized his Neanderthal aesthetic. Red pimples pockmarked his face, either an early sign of puberty or an indication this was not his first attempt at the sixth grade.

Varying shades of brown and yellow stained his white polo shirt, and his blue slacks were faded at the knee. His was the same white polo shirt and blue slacks everyone wore to school. It was the Philadelphia School District uniform, and it was as imaginative as the school itself.

The other boy was Ben Ellis. Ben wore a red hoodie and had a pair of thick, black-rimmed glasses. He eagerly played the part of Shack's Yes Man. By his size and stature, Rian figured self-preservation forced him to accept that role.

"They're called implants," Rian replied.

"Implants? Like they're implanted in your head?" Shack laughed, intending the statement to be an insult. Ben laughed on cue, but the question was actually on target.

6

"Well, yeah. Sort of. I mean, these are magnetic," Rian reached behind her head and pulled a small round disk off the base of her skull. A wire ran from the disk-shaped transmitter to something that looked like a hearing aid, tucked behind her ear.

The moment she removed the cochlear implant, the symphony of screaming children, bouncing balls, and chirping birds changed from a stereo to a mono signal. Without her implants, Rian was completely deaf. When she wore them she was "normal." That's what she used to tell herself, but lately she realized that was not the right word.

When they were on, she was able to hear.

Day one and Rian was already answering questions about the implants. She hated explaining her hearing loss. People always asked questions, but they never understood the answers. Even at Simmons, her old school, she explained her implants to people so often her answers felt scripted.

"They're called cochlear implants. They are not hearing aids. They do not make things louder," she would explain. "I need them to hear. Without them I am hearing impaired."

This was the point where kids would usually ask about something specific that she couldn't hear.

You mean you can't hear a truck?

You mean you can't hear a lawnmower?

You mean you can't hear me making this sound (insert obnoxious fart sound produced by blowing your lips over your forearm)?

The same answer always followed.

No.

Rian was born with a profound hearing loss in both ears, and when she was six months old she got her first cochlear implant.

The auburn-colored disk matched her curly red hair, which she used to keep in pigtails. At age seven she got her second implant. Now she preferred to keep her hair down to hide them. She regretted the decision to wear her hair up today, but it was just so hot when she got out of bed this morning.

"These are my processors. The implant is in my head." Rian held out the processor to show Shack. He reached out to take it from her, and she pulled back abruptly. She returned the device back behind her ear and pressed the round magnetic transmitter to her head.

"That's so weird. You have a magnet in your head. Magnet Head!" Shack's mocking tone was punctuated by prepubescent cracks in his voice.

"Magnet Head!" Ben parroted Shack's insult, speaking for the first time.

"So you're one of them." Shack was clearly more interested in teasing her than in learning about cochlear implant technology.

"Excuse me?" Rian asked.

"I couldn't tell at first. You speak okay, but you are deaf, right?" Shack asked.

"No, I'm hearing impaired." Rian shot back. She did not like to be called deaf. Sure, without the implants she couldn't hear a sound, but unless she was asleep, they were always on her head. She preferred to use the term "hearing impaired." It is what her mother told people, and she thought it described her situation just fine.

"I guess I need to talk like this. Does this help?" As he spoke, Shack flailed his hands and arms as if he were shooing away a swarm of bees.

"Should I talk slow-er so you un-der-stand me?" Ben asked with a mocking tone.

"I'm not deaf!" Rian shot back. In her mind Rian meant to speak forcefully, but the desperation in her voice betrayed her.

She turned her back to them both and started to walk away. It was obvious to her that these boys were trying to bully her, and her father always told her if someone is bullying you the first thing you need to do is walk away. If they don't stop, then you have to punch them in the mouth.

Rian couldn't imagine ever punching someone in the mouth. It was not in her nature. She could handle walking away though.

Shack, feeling disrespected, slipped his fingers behind the wires in her implants and yanked. In one motion, he snatched the processors off her head and was now holding them in his hands.

The immediate silence that followed struck Rian. One of the recess aides was blowing a whistle just before Shack took her processors. Instantaneously, the blaring noise disappeared, along with every other sound in the yard. She whipped around.

"Give them back!" she demanded. Her red face matched her fire-red hair.

Shack said something, but Rian heard nothing. It was as if someone had pressed the mute button on the world. She could see from Shack's idiotic expression and gyrating limbs he was mocking her. Ben was doubled over laughing.

Rian was frightened and angry. She was used to taking her cochlear implants off at night and the silence that came with that routine, but she was never without them outside the safety of her house. She felt panic taking hold. "Give them back!" she shouted again.

Shack dangled the implants in front of her, daring her to take them. She lunged toward him a couple of times. Ben cheered as Shack pulled them away.

On her third attempt, Rian got hold of one of the round disks. She pulled one way as Shack pulled the other, and the wire snapped.

They both stood frozen. Shack looked at the piece in his hand, and Rian looked at the other piece in hers. After a moment, he reached out and handed it back to Rian, along with the other implant.

"You ripped your wire," he insisted.

Rian slipped the left implant back behind her ear and placed the magnet to her head.

Ben laughed mightily. Shack turned and punched him in the arm.

"Shut up, man. It's not funny. She broke her hearing aid. She's deaf. She needs that jawn to hear. You broke your hearing aid," Shack said to Rian as he backed away. "Come on, Ben. Let's go before she starts crying."

Shack and Ben ran to line up with the rest of their class. Rian stood motionless staring at her broken right implant.

2

LUIS RODRIGUEZ

Luis Rodriguez had just fallen asleep when the front right tire of the school bus crashed into a pothole gored deep into Roosevelt Boulevard. The yellow beast convulsed, sending shockwaves through the steel body of the vehicle and into Luis's teeth.

Normally, Luis would catch a little extra sleep on his ride to school. The trip from his home in Rhawnhurst to Millbrook Park was a long one. Except for a few weeks early in the fall, and late in the spring, it was always dark when he boarded the bus.

That morning, he didn't notice Sandra Alfaro sitting across from him until his nap abruptly ended.   She, like Luis, didn't live in Millbrook Park. They were outsiders at John Hancock Elementary School, and they were treated accordingly.

Hancock had special programs for kids like Luis and Sandra. Luis went to Hancock because it was home to a program for Deaf and Hard of Hearing students. He had his own teacher of the deaf, Miss Hughes, and a sign language interpreter, Mr. Rose, who followed him around all day.

Sandra did not have a hearing loss. She was diagnosed with something called Emotional Disturbance. She was given that label after destroying a Smart Board at her old school. A disagreement with her fourth-grade teacher ended with a chair flung across the room and at the board, smashing its screen and rendering it useless. The school's action was swift and decisive. Sandra was kicked out of Ellison Elementary and enrolled at Hancock almost immediately.

Luis liked Sandra. He had barely noticed her in fifth grade, but for some reason this year he found himself staring at her during those long morning bus rides. She was pretty with long dark hair rolling past her narrow shoulders, and she had eyes so dark they trapped light like black holes. She was Dominican, and her light brown complexion matched his own.

There was something else about her that got his attention. She had only one arm. Her right forearm, just below the elbow was missing. She did not wear a prosthetic, choosing instead to function with only her left hand.

This was a condition she was born with and undoubtedly played a role in the way she got along with other people. Sandra was tough. She didn't put up with people she didn't like, and she made instant judgments about people's worthiness. Most did not fare well. Unfortunately for Luis, he was one of those people.

As a member of the Deaf community, Luis wasn't able to talk to Sandra. He didn't speak, and she didn't sign. That was typical for Luis with most of his peers at Hancock. That didn't bother him though. He cared little for the hearing kids in his class. Outside of school, he had plenty of Deaf friends. At school he had friends too. Hassan and Wayne. They were his boys, and that was all he needed.

When he was in fourth and fifth grade, Luis spent many nights trying to convince his mother to send him to the Pennsylvania School for the Deaf. PSD, as it was known, was a school full of kids like Luis. Signers. At a school like PSD, he would be important. A big man among his peers. The role he knew he was born to play.

His mother, Jennifer, wasn't interested in sending him to PSD. It was a residential school, which meant Luis would have to live there during the week. It was also in Germantown, which was far from Rhawnhurst, the part of the city he called home.

Neither Hassan nor Wayne was Deaf like Luis. They were not a part of the Deaf community. Hassan's family emigrated from Pakistan. His parents did not sign, and until two years ago, neither did he. Now, he was practically fluent.

Wayne was from Northwest Philadelphia. Like Hassan, no one in his family was deaf or knew how to sign. The only adult in Wayne's home was his grandmother, who didn't have time to learn to sign. She didn't need to learn. Despite his severe hearing loss, Wayne spoke beautifully. At twelve years of age, he was totally self-sufficient. He made his own meals, cleaned his own clothes and traveled the city all on his own, courtesy of a Septa TransPass that permitted him to ride the bus, trolley or train at all times. Luis envied the freedom Wayne enjoyed.

Luis, Hassan, and Wayne were the three amigos. They ate lunch together, they worked on class assignments together, and they got pulled from class by their teacher of the Deaf together. They hung out at recess together. They were members of the most exclusive club in the school. The Outsiders. On most days, they were all Luis needed.

"What are you staring at?" Sandra asked Luis aggressively.

He turned away, not hearing what she said but getting the message nonetheless. He kept his eyes forward and stared at the cryptic messages scrawled on the back of the vinyl green bus seats that read: *It's hopeless, lil Sweet, its jaboy chips ahoy,* and *Teena Sux.* Sandra reached across the aisle and hit Luis in the arm. He turned and saw her holding out a blank worksheet with twelve unanswered fraction problems.

The gesture confused him. He placed his fist in the palm of his opposite hand and with questioning eyes signed, *Help?*

Sandra's face pinched tightly as she asked, "What?"

Luis took the paper from her and pulled a pencil out of the small front zipper compartment on his Fila backpack. He scooted to the edge of the seat and swung his legs into the aisle. Then, he pulled a Superman graphic novel out of his bag and laid the math sheet on top.

Watch, he signed, pointing his index and middle fingers at Sandra and then turned them to himself.

Question number 1 required you to divide two fractions. He pointed to the sheet with the same two fingers, one on the numerator, and the other on the denominator. With a quick motion he twisted his wrist, reversing his fingers and signed, *Switch.*

13

Sandra watched Luis with equal parts intrigue and annoyance. She wasn't looking for a lesson, just an answer.

"You're drawlin'," Sandra said, the upturned corners of her mouth betraying her frustration with just a hint of a smile. "Gimme that."

Sandra snatched the paper from Luis and placed it in the crux of her right arm. She pointed at it with her left hand. Her index finger, painted with purple nail polish, tapped the sheet then pointed back at Luis.

"Your paper!" she said with wide eyes staring him down.

Luis grabbed his backpack and unzipped the top, pulled out a binder, and removed a completed copy of the same worksheet.

"Give it," Sandra said impatiently, waving her hand in his direction.

Luis obeyed. She took it out of his hand and began copying his answers onto her paper.

He watched as she held the paper to her binder with the stub of her right arm and scribbled away with her left. He wondered if she was naturally left handed or if she would have been right handed if she had a right hand. Could everyone learn to write as beautifully as Sandra with their left?

She turned to him and asked, "What are you starin' at?"

He turned away and looked out the window. The bus raced up a six-lane boulevard with buildings so close to the road an outstretched hand could almost touch them. The passing urban scenery replaced one structure for another, from an apartment complex to a strip mall to a car dealership to a Greek restaurant.

He knew this route cold by now. They passed a police station. Next came a giant statue of a lumberjack pouring syrup from a pitcher in his left hand onto a plate of hotcakes in his right. Next, a series of small two-story homes with long wrap-around porches darted past the window. A bright yellow house, a blue house, and a dingy green house with a towel masquerading as a window shade flew past in that order.

A hand clasped his arm. Luis turned and saw Sandra, holding out his homework sheet. He reached for it and saw that she had only copied the answers. He took the paper and pointed to the directions. Written in all caps and in dark bold print were the words "SHOW YOUR WORK".

"Pshhh," she said, snatching the paper once again from Luis.

Hastily she copied his work in each blank white square. She needed the rest of the ride to finish, and as the bus pulled to a stop and the riders got up to exit, she remained seated for another few moments to complete the job.

Luis waited anxiously for his paper. He turned and looked around, nervous that someone would see what Sandra was doing. No one cared.

"Here," she said, tossing the paper back to him.

She grabbed her bag, slung it over her shoulder, and bolted off the bus. Luis removed his binder from his bag, opened up his math folder, and slipped the sheet back into the sleeve.

That's when he noticed the note. A single word written at the top of the paper. An unexpected show of appreciation but more than that. A flirtation.

On the upper right corner of the homework sheet, just over the date, Sandra had written the word '*Thanks.*' The word was followed by two exclamation points at the end.

The exclamation points were not typical straight lines punctuated by puny dots. Not these exclamation points. These exclamation points had hearts drawn at the bottom. There was a half circle beneath the hearts too. The combination of doodles resembled a smile. Luis got her to say thank you to him. He got her to smile. He tucked the sheet back in his folder and strutted off the bus, ready for the day.

3

AUNT NANCY'S

Rian stood outside Aunt Nancy's house. From the bottom of the steep concrete steps, she stared up at the front door. This was where she lived, but it wasn't her home. Her home was back in Penn Hills. She looked at a sapling in the yard no taller than her, and thought about her maple tree.

Her father, Jack, used to climb up the tree and hide in the branches whenever they played ghosts in the graveyard, something Rian loved to do on a summer's night, when her Aunt Kate and Uncle Aaron came to visit with the cousins.

This house was nothing like that house. Her parents sold that house after the divorce, and now she lived here, in her Aunt Nancy's duplex.

Rian thought Nancy's house was ugly. A conjoined twin, attached to its ugly twin brother. There was no yard to speak of. Everything in Millbrook Park was either made of brick, cement or asphalt, and every home in Millbrook Park, all 200 of them, looked exactly the same. Some were worse off than others, but basically they were all different versions of the same model.

She walked up the front steps, one foot plodding in front of the other. When she got to the top she opened the door.

Her mother, Joanna, was sitting on the couch yelling at someone on her cell phone. Realizing Rian had entered the room, she lowered her voice.

"It's too old," Joanna emphasized each word individually, trading volume for a punctuated emphasis on each syllable.

Joanna got up and left the room, obviously trying to prevent Rian from hearing any more of the conversation. It didn't work.

"There is no warranty. It's too old. The insurance is not going to cover it. Well, you better find some, because this is our responsibility. Yours and mine. I have to go, she just got home. I will call you back later. Well tell her it can wait. This is about our daughter! Ugh." Rian heard Joanna from the next room.

He didn't ask to talk to me, Rian thought to her herself.

"Come here, sweetheart," Joanna walked into the room and toward Rian with her arms open. Rian didn't move. She stood still and braced for her mother's hug.

She thought of how her dad used to call out "family hug" like a train conductor announcing a stop. Her mom and dad would wrap themselves around Rian and each other. It made her feel safe, as if their arms were an impenetrable wall, protecting her from the outside world.

The thought made the reality of her new situation even more painful. Would she ever get another family hug?

"I'm sorry, Mom," she couldn't hold back any longer. Tears welled up in her big hazel eyes and rolled down her freckled cheeks.

"The school told me everything. This wasn't your fault, kiddo." Joanna ran her hand over Rian's head, her fingers getting caught in red ringlets.

"We can't afford it. I don't need another processor. I can hear fine with just one," Rian said.

"Nonsense," Joanna replied, "we will get it repaired, and it will be as good as new."

"How are we supposed to do that? I heard you say—"

"Don't worry about what I said. Your job isn't to worry, that's my job. It will take a little time, but we will get you back online. I promise."

Joanna spoke assuredly, but she knew it was going to be difficult. She had fought the insurance companies before. They were ruthless.

When Rian was seven, Joanna spent weeks calling her surgeon and her insurance company about getting Rian's second implant. She lost her temper with a woman from the insurance company when she said cochlear implants were not a medical necessity.

"How absurd," Joanna blasted into the phone. "My child's ability to hear isn't necessary?"

With her one good ear, Rian heard footsteps coming down the stairs. It was Aunt Nancy.

"Is that Ri?" she asked as she reached the landing.

"Hey, Aunt Nancy," Rian said, wiping the tears from her face.

"I heard your first day sucked pretty hard," Nancy said, getting to the heart of an issue. The bluntness of her comment made Rian chuckle.

"Yeah, it sucked."

"I'm sure you'll get him back. I mean, the jerk who broke your hearing aid." said Aunt Nancy.

"Nancy. It's not a hearing aid, and it's not Rian's job to get him back," Joanna snapped.

"Well, she should. He sounds like a little creep."

"Actually, he's huge," said Rian.

Joanna and Nancy looked at Rian, unsure what to make of the comment. When Rian started laughing, Joanna and Nancy laughed with her. It felt good.

"There you go. Trust me, things will get better. Every dog has its day," Nancy's words were comforting if not confusing.

"Beautiful analogy, Nance," said Joanna. "She's no dog; this boy Gerry Shack, he's the dog."

"He sounds like a pig, but that's not the point. Besides, it's a perfectly reasonable analogy."

18

"What does that mean?" asked Rian.

"It means different things to different people, but you'll know when it applies." Nancy's answer was unclear and unsatisfying.

"What does it mean to you?" Rian asked.

"Me? Well, okay. Do you remember David?" Nancy asked.

"No," replied Rian.

"Sure you do. David. Tall, dark hair, wore t-shirts everywhere." Nancy gestured to show how tall David was, in the hope of sparking Rian's memory.

"Sorry, Aunt Nancy." Rian's memory was not jogged.

"So he and I used to date. The Christmas party two years ago? He had too many—"

"Nancy," Joanna interrupted.

"Sorry. We went out for a while. I liked him a lot. I thought he liked me too. Then one day, he just up and dumped me."

"He dumped you?" Rian asked incredulously.

"Can you believe it? Everything was going great until his ex-girlfriend Sandy came calling. I was devastated. I sat in the house for two weeks wondering what I did wrong."

"What did you do wrong?" asked Rian.

"That's just it. I did nothing wrong. He did. A few weeks after dumping me, Sandy dumped him. She found someone else more interesting than David, and that was that," Nancy insisted.

"I'm still not sure I understand," Rian admitted.

"After she broke up with him, he tried to get back with me. It was my turn to break his heart. It was my day." Nancy spoke proudly.

"In other words, Ri, your Aunt Nancy is the dog in this story." Joanna laughed as she spoke. Nancy threw a hot pair of eyes at her sister.

"In other words, I got my revenge, and so will Rian," Nancy rubbed her hands through Rian's curly hair.

"How?" asked Rian.

"I don't know, but when the time is right, you'll get your chance. Trust me."

Joanna, Nancy and Rian spent the rest of the night eating takeout from a place called Nino's and watching a movie about a man stuck on a deserted island. It was almost enough to make her feel better. If only for the night.

4

PERMISSION

Luis walked beneath the L tracks heading toward the Erie-Torresdale station with his father, Julio, and baby brother, Emilio. Emilio desperately tried to pull away from his father to inspect a large subway poster plastered to a shelter covering the enclosed train platform stairs just up ahead. Despite clutching grocery bags in one hand and Emilio in the other, Julio kept Luis by his side.

The poster that caught Emilio's attention featured a Black woman with caramel-colored skin wearing a yellow bodysuit. She sported an enormous afro and was laughing at something on her white cell phone. The phone was turned toward her, so whatever made her laugh was left up to the imagination.

Luis, imitating the woman in the poster, held his own phone to his face and laughed. His father had given it to him last month. It was slow, and the battery didn't hold a charge, but Luis loved it all the same.

Luis's parents were both Deaf. Emilio, the doctors had said, was hearing. He showed no signs of hearing loss in his newborn screening. This came as a shock to Luis's parents, who had three other children, all of whom were Deaf. They held out hope that the doctor was wrong, but since turning two, Emilio had begun speaking. Hope was fading fast.

Overhead the slow rumble of an approaching train shook the steel girders surrounding them. Luis and Julio could feel the vibrations. Emilio put his hands over his ears as the noise grew louder and louder. Julio grabbed Luis's arm as they ran to catch the train.

When they arrived home, they were greeted by the tangy aroma of sautéed garlic, jalapenos, and green peppers. Jennifer, Luis's mother, was busy frying empanadas on the ancient electric stove in their little galley kitchen. Steam from a frying pan filled the first floor of the small condominium with a heavy arid heat as the sound of sizzling ground meat met only Emilio's ears.

Empanadas were Luis's favorite.

In the living room, Luis's brothers, Miguel and Ricky, pounded their thumbs into dueling PlayStation controllers, each trying to dominate the other in *NBA 2018*. The cheer of the digital crowd and distorted commentary of virtual sportscasters rattled out of a well-worn television speaker.

Emilio ripped free from his father and ran full speed toward his favorite toy, a tiny red toddler table with four large buttons on top creating a ring inside the center. He slapped the four large buttons indiscriminately, playing a melody that could only be tolerated by an audience such as this.

Luis, disappointed that his brothers were already on the PlayStation, turned his attention to his backpack, which he tossed into a corner of the living room. He opened the zipper and pulled a stack of paper out of the bag, one sheet at a time until he found the bright green sheet with an image of a basketball and hoop printed in the center.

It was a permission slip to join the Northeast Philadelphia Junior Basketball League—an interleague athletic group, made up of six local elementary schools, each with its own basketball team. For the first time, Hancock was a member of the league, and permission slips were sent home for interested students wanting to join.

Clutching the paper in his fist, Luis entered the tiny kitchen to show it to his mother. The kitchen was separated from the rest of the condo by a half wall partition. The space between the half wall and the L-shaped counter was no wider than three feet, a very tight space for Jennifer to prepare the family dinner. It was precisely for this reason that she did not want her children to bother her while she made dinner.

Luis was too excited to care about the rule tonight. He needed his mother's permission to join the league, and he was going to get it! He asked his father earlier, when they were shopping, and he gave Luis his usual response, *Ask-mom*.

Jennifer had her back to Luis as he entered her kitchen. She was busy folding the pastry wraps around the sweet hot empanada meat when she felt a tug at her blouse.

With her back to him, Jennifer's right hand flew up over her head.

Go! she signed impatiently.

Refusing to quit that easily, Luis once again pulled on her shirt. He understood the risks of bothering his mom while she made dinner, but this basketball league was worth it.

Sighing deeply, Jennifer finished dimpling a pastry wrap and turned to him. She said nothing. The tilt of her head and the widening of her dark brown eyes sent the message that he'd better make it quick.

Luis thrust the crumpled green paper into her hand. She held it out in front of her, looking past the paper and directly at her son. Luis dropped his eyes to the floor and Jennifer rolled her eyes down to read the sheet.

Six seconds later she gave it back to Luis with the same vigor he used to hand it to her.

No, she signed, snapping her fingers shut.

Not-fair, Luis replied, crashing the tips of his fingers together.

Who-will bring-you? Jennifer asked.

Her questions seemed like an interrogation. *No one needs to bring me. If she actually read the paper, she would know that*, Luis thought to himself.

It's after-school! Luis signed in desperation.

Get-home-how? Jennifer continued.

Train, Luis signed back, heatedly.

The train-is not-safe, Jennifer signed with more concern, noticing her son getting upset.

He pounded his fist into the center of his chest.

Do it-myself! he signed defiantly.

Jennifer just shook her head at the suggestion and turned back to her empanadas. Luis could feel the anger welling up inside. It was like the L train, rumbling the steel girders in his bones.

He slapped his hand on the counter. Jennifer ignored it so he repeated the act three more times. Finally she turned around.

Please, Luis begged, desperately rolling his open palm in the center of his chest.

Jennifer shook her head no and turned back to the empanadas.

Luis balled up the green paper and tossed it over the half wall into the living room. He stomped out of the kitchen, his steps so heavy everyone in the house felt them.

That night, Luis chose to stay in his room and skip dinner. As he felt the empty churning in his stomach, he realized that he succeeded in punishing himself and nothing more. Discouraged and hungry, he fell asleep still wearing his school uniform.

5

MISS CUES

The next day, Rian hid in the coatroom, a walled off section of the class for students to stow their belongings. She was trying to avoid Shack. She spent the night replaying that moment when he held her broken implant in his meaty paws. She scanned the students' backpacks, hanging from hooks fastened to a cinderblock wall and wondered which one belonged to Shack.

"You lost or something?" Sandra, the only other person in the coat room, broke Rian's trance with her question.

"Lost? No." Rian replied hesitantly. Her eyes were immediately drawn to Sandra's missing arm.

"What are you looking at?" Sandra asked aggressively.

"Rian. Rian Radigan," a voice carried from the other side of the wall.

Her teacher, Mrs. Bae-Huley, was loudly calling out Rian's name. Gripping the attendance sheet, Mrs. Bae-Huley scanned the list of names and again called out, "Rian Radigan. Where are you, sweetie?"

"That's me," Rian said to Sandra as she quickly exited the coat closet.

She noticed right away that Shack's desk was vacant. He was absent! A sense of relief washed over her as she made a beeline for Mrs. Bae-Huley's desk.

Mrs. Bae-Huley was Rian's homeroom teacher. She was also her English teacher and Social Studies teacher. This was another reason Rian hated Hancock. At Penn Hills, sixth grade was a middle school grade. Here, sixth grade was still considered elementary school.

Hancock used a system called departmentalization. That was a fancy word that meant she had two teachers instead of one. Her other teacher was Mr. Herman. He was responsible for Math and Science. Rian missed both classes yesterday due to her visit with the principal, Mr. Tasker. She had spent the afternoon in his office, explaining what happened. It was likely the reason for Shack's day off.

Mrs. Bae-Huley was a slender Black woman in her early fifties. Her no-nonsense demeanor was punctuated by tortoise shell glasses sporting a chain that ran behind her head from temple to temple. She wore a gray pencil skirt and a white blouse, with a frilly ruffle running down the front. She looked like a relic from a bygone era.

"Rian, why didn't you come when I called you?" asked Mrs. Bae-Huley. "You having trouble hearing me, child? I thought those implants cured deafness."

"No, I'm not deaf—"

"No need to explain. I'll talk slow," and she did. Very slowly. Mrs. Bae-Huley spoke so slowly, in fact, it was hard for Rian not to laugh.

"You. Need. To. See. Miss Hughes. She. Is. In. Room. Two. Twelve."

"Who?" asked Rian.

"Mrs. Hughes. She. Is. Your. Deaf. Teacher." Mrs. Bae-Huley was practically yelling now.

"I'm not deaf," Rian repeated.

"Go on, sweetheart," Mrs. Bae-Huley said while making a shooing motion with her hand.

Rian was finished with this conversation. She had no idea who Miss Hughes was, but she was needed in room 212. That was good enough for her. She grabbed her stuff and headed out.

Rian exited Mrs. Bae-Huley's room, room 204, and turned left. When she passed room 203, she assumed she was moving in the wrong direction. The hallway curved around a bend in front of her and behind her. She remembered the building was shaped like a giant circle. A relic from the 1960s, she could go either way, and eventually she would get to room 212, Miss Hughes's room.

When she got to the room, she opened the door and found a woman using sign language with a group of boys wearing hearing aids. The scene startled Rian, and for a moment, she thought she was in the wrong room. She turned to the blue placard on the wall with the numbers 212 engraved in white. It was the right room.

"You must be Rian," said Miss Hughes, turning her attention away from her lesson.

Miss Hughes was new to Hancock. In fact, she was new to teaching altogether. She was twenty five years old and could easily still be mistaken for a teenager. Her skin was a radiant chestnut brown color, and her hair bounced as thick black twists, colored purple at the tips, cascaded down past her shoulders. Her face glowed when she smiled at Rian.

Rian recognized the boys from her class. She didn't know their names, but she knew who they were. They were the deaf kids. The ones who needed sign language to communicate.

Suddenly, it occurred to Rian why she was sent here. Miss Hughes was the "hearing teacher." Rian had a hearing teacher in her old school too. Her name was Mrs. Gray and she was older than the steam engine.

Next to Miss Hughes was Mr. Rose. He was young too, but not as young as Miss Hughes. He sat upright, prim and proper. His jet black hair was gelled to a crisp. His white button-down shirt with thin red stripes was starched as stiff as his posture. He was a short man with a boyish face, sitting with his legs crossed.

As Miss Hughes read, Mr. Rose's hands danced wildly in the space beside her. He was a sign language interpreter. Rian was instantly fascinated. All her life people assumed she knew how to sign. Watching Mr. Rose, for the first time she wished she did.

Luis's attention moved from Miss Hughes and Mr. Rose to Rian. He was excited at first when he heard another deaf student was coming to Hancock. It didn't even matter that she was a girl.

His excitement was short-lived however. The moment Luis saw Rian's cochlear implant, his interest vanished and was replaced with resentment. Luis didn't like a lot of people, and he especially took issue with cochlear implant users.

Luis believed implant users were fake deaf.

"Tell us all about you, Rian," Miss Hughes urged, speaking with a warm and welcoming tone. When she spoke, she signed for herself.

"I'm Rian," Rian said.

"Yes, we know that for sure. We're pleased to meet you." said Miss Hughes.

"No we're not," said Wayne.

"Wayne, be polite. Rian is a new friend. A member of our team. We need to welcome her to Hancock."

There was an empty seat next to a boy named Hassan. Hassan had light brown skin and dark brown hair. He was very tall. The only boy in class taller than Hassan was Shack, but Hassan was not oafish. He was upright and slender.

"Have you had a chance to meet the crew?" Miss Hughes asked.

"No." said Rian nervously.

"You'll need a name sign," Miss Cues said, signing each individual letter in her name.

Luis crossed his fingers, making the sign for the letter *R* and tapped it behind his ear. Wayne and Hassan laughed. Rian wasn't sure why it was funny, but she was smart enough to figure out that he was making fun of her implants.

"I don't know how to sign." Rian's words sounded like a confession or admission of guilt. Something about being in this room with these boys made her feel even more out of place than being in Mrs. Bae-Huley's room.

"You don't have to sign. Mr. Rose can do that for you. Tell us where you're from?" Miss Hughes spoke with kindness in her voice. Rian wanted to talk to her. She didn't care at all about these boys, but she wanted to know Miss Hughes.

"Okay, I just moved here from Penn Hills."

As she spoke, her eyes remained glued to Mr. Rose. She was fascinated, watching him translate her words into signs.

"Talk to them, not me," said Mr. Rose.

"What?" asked Rian.

"When I am signing for you, you don't look at me. I am your voice. You look at the people you are addressing," replied Mr. Rose.

"Okay," she said, forcing herself to stop looking his way.

"I used to go to Simmons Elementary school. I've been hearing impaired my whole life…"

Luis mimicked Mr. Rose's sign for *hearing impaired*, mocking Rian.

"Hearing impaired?" Mr. Rose voiced sarcastically, matching Luis's facial expression.

Rian's attention swung from Luis to Mr. Rose and back to Luis.

Miss Hughes jumped in, "What Luis is trying to say is we don't use the term 'hearing impaired' in here."

"Well, I do. I mean, I'm not deaf."

Luis signed using very large motions. Once again, Mr. Rose voiced for him, "That's right. You're not Deaf."

"You have a profound hearing loss," said Miss Hughes. "Without your implants, you hear nothing. That makes you deaf. The term 'hearing impaired' suggests that something is broken. None of you are broken. You are all wonderful and unique."

Rian was not convinced, but she was willing to listen.

"It's our turn. Why don't we introduce ourselves? Let's start with you, Wayne." Said Miss Hughes.

"No," Wayne said, glaring at Rian.

"We're going to work together all year. We should at least get to know each other," replied Miss Hughes.

"We are? I mean, I am going to be working in here? With them?" Rian asked, the incredulous look now belonging to her.

Hassan raised his hand, "I will talk Miss Cues…" Rian chuckled at Hassan's mispronunciation of Miss Hughes's name, offending him.

"Rian, we don't laugh at each other in here," said Miss Hughes.

"I'm sorry," said Rian. "I wasn't laughing at him, but he said miscues."

"Yes," said Miss Hughes. "It can be hard for some of us to pronounce specific words that use specific sounds. Especially when you can't hear those sounds."

"I mean, a miscue is a mistake. He used the word 'mistake' in his mistake. It's a pun!" said Rian, very proud of her understanding of puns.

"I suppose you're right, but it still isn't polite. Go ahead, Hassan," Miss Hughes said, throwing her smile his way.

"My name is Hassan Alvi. I am Pakistan—"

"Pakistani," Miss Hughes corrected him.

"Pakistan-ee," Hassan over-emphasized the last sound. "I am killed with soccer. I play soccer when I grow up."

"Watch Hassan," Miss Hughes said leaning in to Hassan and pointed to her mouth. "Skilled in soccer."

"I am skilled in soccer," he repeated, overemphasizing the *S* sound in both words.

Hassan's speech was startling to Rian. She wasn't used to hearing someone speak with such a pronounced deaf intonation. His voice sounded monotone, adding inflection on the wrong syllables of words. Hassan was not a native English speaker. His parents were immigrants, and his first language was Urdu, which impacted his grammar.

"Nice to meet you," said Rian uneasily.

"Watch," Miss Hughes said, bringing Rian's attention back to her.

Miss Hughes slowly ran her open right palm across her upturned left palm. She then balled her fists and extended the index fingers on either hand.

Moving the right index finger to the left she said, "This is how we sign it. Nice to meet you."

Rian imitated the sign and repeated the comment, *Nice-to meet-you.*

Turning to Luis, Miss Hughes signed, *Your turn.*

Luis turned away from her. She tapped her hand on the table.

Introduce-yourself, she said, signing as she spoke.

Luis peered at Rian with a sideways glance. He snapped his fingers to his thumb, signing, *No!*

"That's not okay. She is a member of our community, and we will treat her that way," Miss Hughes insisted.

She is-not-a member-of our-community. I am-Deaf. Hassan is-Deaf. She is a-CI, Luis signed, as Mr. Rose voiced his words.

She-is d-e-a-f, Luis finger spelled the last word. *We are-capital-D-e-a-f.*

"I don't understand," Rian said, confused.

Mr. Rose stepped out of his role as interpreter for a moment to explain what Luis meant.

"What Luis is trying to say is he is Deaf with a capital D. That means he is a member of the Deaf community. You are not a member of that community. You are deaf with a lowercase d. Like Miss Hughes said, that means you can't hear without your implants."

Mr. Rose fingerspelled the letters *C* and *I*, but Luis shook his head, waving off Mr. Rose's sign. Luis crashed his index and middle fingers into his skull behind his ear. His fingers however, were separated and bent. When he made the sign, it looked like he were imitating something being plugged into the back of his skull.

Luis Wayne and Hassan laughed out loud. Rian had no idea what was supposed to be funny, but she knew for sure she was the butt of the joke.

Without using her voice, Miss Hughes stood up and signed to the boys with a sternness that startled Rian. Whatever joke Luis made, Miss Hughes wasn't having any of it. The boys stopped laughing, and their expressions soured as she admonished them. When she was finished, all three apologized to Rian, begrudgingly.

Miss Hughes stood up and walked to her desk. She gestured for Rian to follow her. On her desk sat a black speaker, approximately the size of a loaf of bread. There were four knobs on the side of it. Under each nob were words: volume, tone, bass, and treble.

"Do you own an FM system?" asked Miss Hughes.

"No," replied Rian. "I used to borrow one at my old school. I don't have one of my own."

"Well, this is an FM that I need you to use." As she spoke, Miss Hughes pointed to the black speaker on her desk.

"Okay." Rian did not like the looks of the thing.

The FM system Rian used in her old school had a small piece called a boot that plugged into the back of the processor behind her ear. Her teacher wore a microphone, and when she spoke, Rian could hear her teacher's voice as if she were standing right in front of her.

There was no large black speaker that came with her old FM. She didn't know what this thing was.

"This is the receiver," Miss Hughes pointed to the big black speaker. "You will need to keep this close to you. Your teacher or partner will wear this microphone."

Miss Hughes reached into a small black cradle and pulled out a large silver microphone with a thick lanyard looped around it.

"When people speak, their voice will be amplified by the receiver. It will help you while you are waiting for your CI to be repaired."

The thing was a monstrosity. Rian wanted her hearing loss to be hidden from the other students, and this thing was as conspicuous as a giant billboard with a neon green arrow pointed directly at her.

"I don't need that. I'll be fine," Rian said apologetically. It was nice for Miss Hughes to try to help, but this thing was no help. It was the opposite of help.

Miss Hughes slipped the large clunky microphone around her neck and flipped a switch on the side, igniting a bright red light.

"It's not negotiable. You need to use it."

As she spoke, her voice bellowed out of the speaker. Each word felt like an uppercut hitting Rian in the face.

"It will charge in Mrs. Bae-Huley's room, so you can grab it first thing in the morning. It will be your job to charge it at the end of the day. I know it's not ideal, but it will make communication a lot easier. I read your records. It's been a very long time since you've had one working implant. I promise, this will help. Go ahead, take it."

Rian stared at the speaker. She stared at the large silver microphone around Miss Hughes's neck. She grabbed the speaker by its black handle. Miss Hughes then slipped the microphone off her neck and placed it lovingly around Rian's.

"There you go. Rian, I am really looking forward to getting to know you better. We will have a chance to meet, just the two of us, tomorrow after Math class."

Rian stared down at the microphone around her neck.

"Great," she said with no matching enthusiasm. The loudness of her voice amplified through the speaker, startling her.

"You need to get going. Mrs. Bae-Huley is going to wonder what happened to you."

Feeling defeated, Rian headed toward the door. Luis and Wayne laughed. She hated the speaker. For a moment she thought about dropping it on the ground, breaking it and ending the nightmare right then and there.

She didn't need this thing. Why didn't she have a say in this? She knew what she could hear. She knew better than Miss Hughes for sure.

Rian did not drop the speaker on the floor. Instead, she did exactly as she was told. She walked back to Miss Bae-Huley's class and got to work.

6

NORMAL KIDS

Mrs. Bae-Huley walked up and down the aisles of her classroom, dropping large salmon-colored packets on each desk she passed.

"Please write your name on the cover where it says Name," she said as packets continued to flop on desk after desk.

Rian did as she was told.

"Your job today is to choose a state in the continental United States and research that state's motto, bird, capital, chief export, professional sport teams, et cetera, et cetera. We will be working on this for the next few days. You may choose a partner to work with."

Before she finished speaking, the students were capturing one another's wandering eyes and pointing to their partner of choice.

Rian scanned the room, looking for a friendly set of eyes. She refused to look to her left, where Luis, Hassan, and Wayne sat clustered together. Two by two the students paired up nodding and smiling in confirmation of their partnership.

Eventually her eyes landed on Sandra. She was slouched in her seat staring upward at the ceiling. She was not looking for a partner. She appeared to be counting holes in the ceiling tiles.

As if she could feel Rian looking at her, Sandra moved her eyes from the ceiling to Rian, who cautiously nodded her head as an invitation to work together. Sandra dropped her head back and returned her eyes to the ceiling.

35

Unfazed, Rian asked out loud, "Do you want to work together?" assuming Sandra did not understand the purpose of her head nod.

Sandra was caught off guard by Rian's request. It showed on her face but only for a moment.

"No," Sandra said with a shrug.

"We are going to use the laptops," said Mrs. Bae-Huley to an eruption of cheers. "Calm down, boys and girls. One two three, eyes on me." Mrs. Bae-Huley called out.

"One two, eyes on you," the class responded.

"I want everyone to sit silently until I get you your machine. Not a sound." Mrs. Bae-Huley said, making her way over to the laptop cart, a white box on wheels. She turned a key, already jutting out of the lock, and opened it.

There was one computer cart for the entire school. That meant the fourth-, fifth-, and sixth-grade teachers had to share. By the time Mrs. Bae-Huley's turn came around that day, three computers were missing, another two were broken, and four were put back uncharged.

"Jesus, give me the strength," Mrs. Bae-Huley whispered under her breath, assessing the state of the computers.

Despite her attempt to speak quietly, Mrs. Bae-Huley forgot she was wearing both Rian's and Hassan's FM microphones around her neck. Her thoughts on the state of the laptop cart traveled through Rian's speaker, causing her to chuckle.

Mrs. Bae-Huley grabbed a clipboard from the top of the cart and scanned it to find the name of the last teacher who last signed it out. She was unsurprised to see the name Joe Herman just above her own. Technically, what she saw was a shapeless blue line that ran across the page starting from a big obnoxious loop. After sixteen years of working together, she recognized the signature.

"Of course," she said, dropping the clipboard on top of the cart and marching over to a phone hanging on the wall.

She dialed 4314, the extension for Mr. Herman.

Mrs. Bae-Huley's distraction was an immediate invitation for the class to engage in conversations on all kinds of topics. The FM system around her neck remained on, and so despite their disinterest in her phone call with Mr. Herman, Rian and Hassan were again forced to listen to her end of the conversation.

"Joe, it's Cil. Did you just have the laptop cart? It's a mess. I am aware, but there are a number of machines that were put back and not plugged in. How am I supposed to...? It always seems that this is how they are left after you've had them ...

"I would appreciate more consideration for the rest of us who need to use these things, Joe. Not much good that does me. Fine," Mrs. Bae-Huley said hanging up the phone.

She turned her attention back to the class.

"It looks like we will have to work in groups of three today," the frustration in her voice was palpable. "Feel free to group yourselves. Luis, Hassan, and Wayne, you three will work together. Rian, you can work with the boys too."

Rian turned to look at the three of them. Mr. Rose had just finished interpreting Mrs. Bae-Huley's decision to assign her to the group.

Luis turned from Mr. Rose to Rian and snarled. He signed something, flipping his upward facing hands downward in a quick sharp motion.

Mr. Rose voiced for him saying, "We don't want to work with her."

Before Mrs. Bae-Huley could respond, a girl's voice spoke out from the back of the room.

"She can work with us," a voice called out from the back of the room.

Rian turned around and saw that the voice belonged to Elisha Gadson. Elisha was a fair-skinned Black girl sitting in the back row of the classroom.

"I'm sorry Elisha, Rian needs the interpreter…" Mrs. Bae-Huley announced.

"No, I don't. I'm not deaf," Rian replied.

She saw that Elisha was working with another girl, her bestie, Jamilah Massulah.

Thank goodness, Rian thought to herself. *I can work with some normal kids*. The fleeting thought seemed wrong in its bluntness, but Rian didn't care.

"Just make sure you bring your speaker," Mrs. Bae-Huley said, removing the microphone from around her neck.

Rian stared at the speaker disgustedly. Mrs. Bae-Huley turned away, and Rian got up leaving the speaker behind. She had absolutely no intention of asking these girls to wear that microphone. She would hear them just fine, thank you very much.

Students rearranged desks and chairs. There was an empty desk next to Elisha. The desk was to Elisha's left, meaning Rian's deaf ear would be faced toward her. Rian knew it made sense to pull up a chair from a desk in the row in front of the girls, so she could face them, but Elisha tapped her hand on the desk beside her in a way that made it hard for Rian to refuse.

"Sit here," she insisted.

Rian sat at the desk. Elisha was positioned between Rian on her left and Jamilah on her right. Elisha bounced out of her seat to get a laptop.

The moment Elisha got up, an awkward silence settled in between Rian and Jamilah. Feeling pressured to say something, Rian spoke.

"Your scarf is very pretty," she said, admiring the black wrap surrounding Jamilah's head and neck.

"It's a hijab, not a scarf," Jamilah said without looking Rian's way.

"Oh. Okay," Rian said, embarrassed.

Although she felt it best to remain quiet until Elisha returned, Rian couldn't help but make another comment.

"It's very pretty," she said.

"It's not supposed to be pretty. That's not a compliment," Jamilah snapped, turning her body toward Rian this time. The quick movement and rigid posture made it clear that she had enough of this conversation.

"I didn't mean to be rude," said Rian.

"Is it rude for me to ask about your... what is that thing on your head? An earring? A hair braid? Should I just keep guessing?" asked Jamilah.

Rian knew most people knew nothing about implants, but she hated that it was always the first thing they asked about. Never, I love your hair, or where did you get that outfit? Whenever she met someone new, this was the first thing they noticed, and it bothered her to always have to answer that question.

She wondered if that was exactly what Jamilah felt about her hijab.

"It's my implant," she said shyly, hoping there wouldn't be a follow-up question.

"What is an implant?" Jamilah asked, staring at it with bemused fascination. She was trying to see the implant, but it was behind Rian's left ear, which faced away from her.

"It helps me to hear." This was all the explanation Rian was willing to provide. She didn't want to talk about it. She wanted to talk about the project, or whatever these girls normally talked about.

Elisha returned with a computer and placed it on her desk. Jamilah snatched it, opened it, and began typing.

"Hi, Elisha," Rian said excitedly.

"Hi," Elisha said turning to Rian. They smiled at one another before Elisha turned back around to Jamilah who said something to Elisha that Rian did not hear or understand.

"I love your hair," Elisha offered, absolutely making Rian's day.

"Thank you. I love yours too!" Rian gushed.

The room was buzzing with student chatter and clicking computer keys. Some kids were on task looking up information about a state, while others were using the computers for other forms of entertainment.

Elisha looked to see if Mrs. Bae-Huley was paying attention. The teacher sat behind her desk, with her cell phone in her hand, swiping up.

"Do you watch 'Black Pack'?" Elisha asked Rian.

Rian was looking in her backpack for something to write with and didn't notice Elisha talking to her. Mrs. Bae-Huley had a radio behind her desk that was playing something called Moonlight Sonata. She liked to put classical music on when the class was working. She believed it was calming, and that helped students focus.

That was exactly the opposite case for Rian. Between the music and the noise from all the other students, she was struggling to understand Elisha and Jamilah.

"Do you watch 'Black Pack'?" Elisha repeated.

Jamilah was watching a YouTube video of a family playing Russian roulette with a plastic pumpkin. Each family member took turns pressing a pumpkin to their skull. There was a button at the bottom of the pumpkin, that when depressed made a cracking sound. Each time the button was pushed, the person holding the pumpkin closed their eyes in anticipation of a gush of water to stream out and soak their head. Most of the time nothing happened, but every few turns, someone got wet.

"Sure, I watch 'Backpack,'" Rian said, lying for no reason.

Jamilah laughed. "She said 'Black Pack.' It's the name of the family, the Blacks. There are six of them: Liam, Brayden, Grayson, Livy, Lhasa, and Meredith."

"Right," Rian replied, "'Black Pack,'" and she over-emphasized the word *black*.

Jamilah turned to Elisha and said something. Rian thought she saw her mouth the word *dumb*, but she wasn't sure. Lots of words looked like the word *dumb* when you're lip reading—like *lamb* and *numb*. Besides, Rian didn't lip read all that well.

"Shouldn't we get started?" asked Rian.

"We're fine. She's not even paying attention," said Elisha, pointing to Mrs. Bae-Huley, who stopped swiping and was now reading something on her phone.

"We're going to run out of time." Rian said nervously. She did not like being off task. It was not in her nature. She was an A student, and she didn't get to be an A student by goofing off.

Jamilah rolled her eyes and peered in Rian's direction, "Whatever," she said as she opened a new tab.

"What state should we choose?" Elisha asked.

"How about Wyoming!" Rian answered, pleased they were back on track.

"Wyoming?" Jamilah asked incredulously. "Why Wyoming?"

"It's beautiful there. My dad used to live there. He's going to take me there someday. To see Yellowstone. It's a park on a giant super volcano!" Rian's excitement about Wyoming was completely lost on her partners, but they weren't about to pick a different state, so Wyoming was the winner.

Jamilah typed the word *Wyoming* into the search bar. The first page that came up was a Wikipedia page. She clicked on it.

"I know a good place to find information on states," Rian said to Jamilah. "It has all the facts listed, and they're easy to find."

"This will work. Wikipedia knows everything," Jamilah replied without taking her eyes off the screen.

"My old teacher told me Wikipedia is unreliable. People can change information anytime. Try state-facts-for-kids-dot-net," Rian continued.

Jamilah turned and said something to Elisha. Elisha chuckled. Rian did not hear what was said, but she had the feeling that was intentional.

41

Elisha took the computer from Jamilah, handed it to Rian, and said, "Here. Show us what you've got."

Jumping at the opportunity to take the lead, Rian hurriedly typed statefactsforkids.net. A colorful, kid-friendly website popped up.

"See, if I click here, I can pick from fifty states on the map. I used this in my old school to research Connecticut." Unfortunately Rian did not pronounce Connecticut correctly. Instead she said connect-eh-cut. This mispronunciation sent Jamilah into hysterics.

"It's called Connecticut."

"Here, let me see it," Elisha said, taking the laptop from Rian's desk and moving it to her own. "How about this, you tell me what to find, and I will find it."

"OK." Rian grabbed the packet and wrote all three girls' names on top. "How do you spell Jamilah," she asked.

"J-A-M-I-L-A-H", said Jamilah.

"One L?" Rian asked for clarification.

Jamilah repeated the letters in her name a second time for Rian. This time she punctuated the spelling of her name by adding a staccato-like over-pronunciation of each letter.

Rian limply wrote Jamilah's name after Elisha's. Then, pretending that didn't just happen, she asked the first question.

"What is the population of Wyoming?"

Elisha scanned a section of the website called Quick Facts and found the answer. "579,000 people."

"What is the official state animal?" Rian asked.

Elisha scanned again, before saying, "Bison."

Rian wrote the answer and moved on to the third question. "What is the capital?"

"Cheyenne," said Elisha.

Rian looked up at Elisha. She was not at all familiar with that word. She looked at Elisha's mouth to make sure she understood her correctly.

"What?" asked Rian.

"Cheyenne," Elisha repeated.

Rian nodded and turned to the packet. She wrote the word '*Kyland*'. She tried to disguise what she was writing from the girls, but Elisha suspected she was confused and looked at the page.

"No—Cheyenne," Elisha said.

Rian immediately started erasing what she wrote, embarrassed by the fact that her mistake was discovered. Worse yet, she still wasn't sure what Elisha said.

"Can you spell it for me?" Rian asked apologetically.

"Never mind," Elisha said.

"If you spell it…"

"Don't worry about it," Elisha replied, "I'll do the writing."

Elisha passed the laptop back to Jamilah and took the packet off Rian's desk. She finished erasing Rian's mistake and wrote the word *Cheyenne*.

Rian didn't know whether to feel embarrassed, upset, or angry. Whatever she felt was a toxic combination of all three. She didn't want the girls to see her upset, so she got up to sharpen her pencil.

As she passed Luis, Wayne, and Hassan, she could see them laughing heartily about something.

Were they laughing at her? She shook off the thought, wondering why she even cared to ask.

It's okay. Elisha will like you as soon as she gets to know you. Just go back there, and have some fun," Rian thoughts returned to her partners. She just needed to give herself a pep talk while sharpening her already pointy pencil.

When she was ready, Rian made an about-face and returned to her partners. She saw Elisha and Jamilah once again watching "Black Pack." They were sharing a set of earbuds and giggling at the video.

Elisha removed her earbud and offered it to Rian. "Want to listen?" she asked.

Rian shook her head no, knowing that was impossible. After that, Rian held her head down the rest of the class and drew a unicorn on her packet, waiting for the lunch bell to ring.

7

HOOP DREAMS

The soft green couch in Luis's apartment was old and battered. A section between the two cushions in the dead center of the sofa had sunken in years ago. Luis loved to nestle himself into that large dimple, which surrounded his legs and arms with the softness of the faded green cushions. From that place, he furiously manned his PlayStation remote and commanded his favorite virtual NBA team, the 76ers, against any rival who dared challenge him. Currently, he was playing his favorite online rival, Hassan.

There weren't many other Deaf kids in Luis's neighborhood. He had plenty of friends that could sign outside of school, but like all things, he depended on his parents for that. Most weekends, Julio and Jennifer would meet up with their Deaf friends and go out to dinner or a movie. Their favorite meetup was bowling. Luis loved to bowl.

There were usually a lot of Deaf people at the weekend meetups. There were always kids, and they always knew how to sign. Even the few hearing kids in the group were fluent because their parents were Deaf. Those kids were called CODAs. That meant they were a child of deaf adults, and they were as much a part of the Deaf community as Luis and his family. Luis loved weekends.

Evenings after school were a different story. Once homework was finished, Luis was usually bored. He loved his PlayStation, but his mother made sure to limit the amount of time he spent on it, and when he was done there wasn't much else to do in their tiny condominium.

There was a basketball court in the complex where he could go to work on his game, but the weather was turning cold, and night was coming earlier. Jennifer did not want Luis to play basketball after dark.

He was capping off another in a string of victories over Hassan, when Jennifer sat on the couch beside him. When the game was over, she picked up the television remote and turned it off. Luis got up, pressed the power button on the PlayStation, and returned to his burrow in the couch.

He sat sullen, still angry at his mother for refusing to allow him to join the basketball team. Jennifer recognized this and the limitations placed on her son. He loved his mother, and she knew that, but she hated when he was cold to her. The only other time he had stayed this upset with her was when she told him he was not allowed to go to the Pennsylvania School for the Deaf.

Jennifer was cautious. It was just her parenting style. Her manner toward Luis was no different than it was toward his older siblings, but there was a difference, and she recognized it. Those two had each other to play with growing up. They were too old now to take much interest in Luis, and his baby brother was too young.

She was afraid to send him to PSD because it was far from their house, and she didn't know a lot of the people who sent their children there.

A devoutly religious woman, Jennifer believed that Deaf people were chosen to be Deaf by God. Hearing people lived in the hearing world and deaf people in a visual world. She believed when a child got a cochlear implant that child was stolen from the Deaf community. It was, in her eyes, a sin against God.

Luis stared at the black screen in front of him, refusing to acknowledge his mother. She placed her hand on his head and ran her fingers, capped with long red nails, gently through the tiny dark curls of hair on his head. The light touch of her fingers to his scalp was a comforting feeling. Many nights, when he couldn't fall asleep, Jennifer would sit on his bed and rub her fingers along the top of his head.

Today, though, Luis jerked away from her, not wanting to be comforted. He was angry, and he planned to stay that way.

Look at me, she signed with a quick twist of her wrist.

With his arms folded across his chest, Luis turned his head to look at his mother.

We-need to-talk, she signed to him.

Luis said nothing. He raised his eyebrows slightly as if to say, go ahead.

Jennifer rotated her right hand in small circles around her temple, rolling the tips of her fingers against her thumb. She wanted to let Luis know she had been thinking about his basketball league.

That got Luis's attention.

I'm-worried-about-you, she signed.

Pulling one folded arm free, Luis jammed his thumb into the center of his chest and signed, *I'm-fine*!

*You're-growing up-fas*t, she replied, moving her hand from her waist to her head, to illustrate her point. *I can't-keep you locked away-forever. I just-love you-very much.*

Luis dropped his chin to his chest, unable, as always, to stay angry with his mother.

Jennifer reached into her pocket and pulled out a badly wrinkled sheet of green paper. She pressed it into her leg with her open palm to smooth out the wrinkles and handed it to him.

Confused, he unfolded the paper and saw to his surprise that she had signed the permission slip. She changed her mind. He was allowed to play basketball!

8

NOT REAL DEAF

Math was a rigid, uncompromising routine played out over a ninety-minute block of time, every day. The teacher, Mr. Herman, was an ashy gray septuagenarian with sporadic white hairs limply disguising his big bald head. He was the most senior teacher at Hancock and the third most senior teacher in Philadelphia. He sang songs to the class that were generations older than him, songs meant to provide a lesson in safety for any child who might climb on a roof or play along the railroad tracks.

Mr. Herman was also a gossip who spent his lunch break dishing on the other teachers with the members of his exclusive inner circle. He loved telling tales of the water-main break of '68 and the great strike of '81. He planned to never leave Hancock. He loved the building and his time in it. The only thing he didn't love at this stage of his career was teaching Math to sixth graders.

Math class always started the same way. Students wrote answers to mental math problems on a dry erase board. Once you finished the problem, you held the dry erase board over your head, which allowed Mr. Herman the opportunity to shame students with the wrong answer.

After that, there was a lesson designed for the Smart Board. The Smart Board in Mr. Herman's room was permanently affixed to a decades-old chalkboard. The chalkboard, not the Smart Board, was used to teach the lesson. Mr. Herman scribbled his notes in the spaces flanking the board. He called the Board useless and insisted it didn't work. He said it was an unnecessary waste of taxpayer money.

After forty minutes of watching Mr. Herman fumble his way through problem after problem, students broke into pairs and practiced the day's lesson in their math journals. The journal was a stew of function boxes, line plots, number stories, and practice problems.

Until today, Rian kept to herself during partner activities. She made no effort to inform Mr. Herman that she had no one to work with, and he made no effort to pair her with anyone. It was, for Rian, the perfect arrangement. Today, however, Wayne's partner, Hector, was absent.

When it was time to pair up, Wayne shot his hand into the air to let Mr. Herman know he had no one to work with. Tilting his head back and surveying the room, Mr. Herman's eyes landed on Rian.

"You," he said, nodding his head in her direction. "What's your name, kiddo?"

Rian tried to pretend she didn't hear him.

"Hello. Red? You with the red hair?" Mr. Herman shuffled a few papers around his desk until he came across a seating chart. He pushed his glasses up the bridge of his nose and scanned the sheet looking for Rian's name.

"Rain. Rain? That's a funny name. Your parents are hippies, eh? So be it. Do you have a partner, Rain?" Mr. Herman asked.

The misreading of Rian's name ignited laughter throughout the room. Rian slunk into her chair and said with absolutely no authority, "My name is Rian."

"What? Rain, you're going to work with Wayne today."

"I don't need a partner" she argued. As she spoke, she looked over at Luis, who was glaring at her.

"Perfect. Work with Wayne." Mr. Herman dropped his head and returned to the catnap he had been enjoying before Wayne interrupted.

Rian turned to look at Wayne. Because of their hearing loss, they both sat in the front row, right next to each other. Wayne was short and skinny, and like many other boys and girls in the class, he was Black.

At her old school, there was one girl in her class who was Black. Her name was Tamara, and she didn't seem much different from the other kids in her class. At Hancock, there were many Black students, maybe more Black students than white students, Rian thought. As if being deaf didn't make her stand out enough, here at Hancock she was a racial minority. This was especially true once you included the Hispanic and Asian students at the school.

Rian assumed Wayne was as disinterested with her as she was with him. She didn't want to risk getting into a conversation with him, so she buried her face in her workbook and got started on page 107. At first, the plan seemed to work. Wayne didn't try to work with her. When she got to the fourth math box, however, she noticed Wayne was copying her answers.

She shifted her journal away from him, but that just made his efforts to copy her work more obvious. He craned his neck to see her page. She switched her pencil to her left hand, and used her right to cover her work. She wasn't left-handed, which made writing a real challenge.

The strategy was too effective. Wayne couldn't see her work any longer so he decided to say something. He tapped her on the arm that covered her work. She turned to look his way.

"Let me look!" he demanded.

"We aren't working together. You are just copying my work. That's cheating," Rian insisted.

Luis and Hassan also sat in the front row of the class. They were on the other side of the room working with Mr. Rose.

"Maybe you should work with them," Rian said, pointing in their direction.

Wayne threw his hand in the air and waved it like a freshly caught fish flopping on the dock of a boat. Mr. Herman looked up from his desk.

"Yes, Wayne?" he asked.

"She's not working with me," he complained.

"He is just copying my work," Rian said defiantly.

"You need to work together," Mr. Herman said with a tone in his voice that expressed complete disinterest in addressing the problem.

"But—" Rian was cut off.

"But nothing, Rain. Wayne is your partner. Make it work."

She looked at Wayne, who was grinning from ear to ear. He made a nodding gesture, throwing his eyes at the journal.

"Fine." Rian pushed the journal over to his desk. Wayne continued to copy Rian's work.   She stared at Mr. Herman coldly. He either didn't notice or didn't care.

When he was done, Wayne returned the journal. Written in the margins at the bottom of the page were three words. The words had been gone over in pencil again and again, darkening each letter to ensure the message was sent loud and clear.

The message read: *NOT REAL DEAF!*

9

CAFETORIUM

Stuck in a slow moving lunch line, Rian stared at her Salisbury steak. She imagined it was a dimpled brown island surrounded by a sea of gravy. The tray she carried was designed to separate the main course from her green beans, mashed potatoes, and cornbread. Despite those intentions, the corn bread was already brown and soggy from gravy that breached the Styrofoam levy.

Gross, she thought to herself.

She reached into a stainless steel chiller and pulled a half pint of Rosenberger's chocolate milk out as she neared the register. From where she stood, Rian could see a seat on the far end of the lunch table directly across from Elisha and Jamilah. She waited all week for a seat to open up near the girls in the hopes of taking another shot at becoming friends with them.

A wave of anxiety washed over her. Getting a good seat at the lunch table was difficult. Her class was large and the lunch tables were not. Twice last week, she had to sit at the misfit table next to the main table. The misfit table was reserved for students who had no one to save them a spot at the main table. It was also where Luis, Wayne, and Hassan sat. She wanted to steer clear of those three. She didn't want people to think she was deaf like them.

A fifth-grade boy in front of Rian moved on, bringing her to the front of the line at last. The lunch lady at the register wore a translucent hairnet, masking her long silver locks. Her eyebrows looked like they were drawn on her face with a felt tip marker and her mouth, painted with bright red lipstick, was pinched into a permanent look of disapproval. Her eyes danced from one item on Rian's tray to the next as she typed the selections onto a screen in front of her.

"Two-fifty," the woman said for likely the three-hundredth time that day.

A little blue machine, resembling a calculator, rested on the stainless steel table separating Rian from the woman. The machine allowed Rian to access her lunch account. All she had to do was type in her eight-digit student identification number and the meal was hers. Her eyes shifted from the empty seat in front of Elisha down to the machine.

Four, nine, six, three, seven, three, eight, six; she typed into the little blue machine.

"Wrong," announced the woman with the hairnet.

The last digit was supposed to be a seven, not a six. The wave of anxiety she felt now seemed to be a rising tide, coming up past her throat. She saw Cierra Shaw, another girl from her class, heading toward the lunch table. She was going to lose the seat.

"Let's go. You're holding up the line!" The lunch lady spoke with an intolerance that could only be cultivated over years of serving sixth graders Salisbury steak.

Telling herself to get a grip, Rian slowly punched in the eight-digit number, hit the green *Enter* button, and completed the sale.

"Have a good one," said the lunch lady, her words trailing off as Rian scooped up her tray and darted to the table. She was about halfway there when Cierra squeezed herself into the seat just across from Elisha. Elisha's face lit up at the sight of her friend and they dove immediately into a conversation.

It wasn't fair. That was supposed to be Rian's conversation. She spent an hour every night last week watching "Black Pack" to prepare for that conversation. She stopped and looked around for another empty seat. Nothing.

Her eyes shifted to the misfit table. There were only five students there, leaving plenty of room for her to sit and eat her Salisbury steak. Luis, Wayne, and Hassan sat clustered at one end of the table. Lucas was a few spots down from the Deaf kids, and Sandra was all alone on the opposite end of the table. Her head was face down in her folded arm. She appeared to be napping.

Feeling dejected, Rian plunked herself down across from Sandra. The thrust of the tray hitting the table was enough to pull Sandra from her sleep. She awoke angry.

"You're outta pocket." she barked at Rian, her eyes half open as they adjusted to the light in the cafeteria.

"Something fell out?" Rian asked, looking at the floor to find what she dropped

"What are you talking about?" said Sandra.

"My pocket. Did you say something fell out of my pocket?" Rian asked.

Laughing, Sandra said, "I said you're out of pocket."

"What does that mean?" asked Rian.

"It means, what's your problem?" Sandra answered.

"Problem?" Rian asked.

"Yeah, what's wrong with you?" she repeated.

"If you're asking about my implant, there's nothing wrong with me, it's just how I hear," Rian replied.

"I'm not talking about that thing. I don't care about your ears. I mean why you so loud? You don't see me trying to sleep?" Sandra's tone was becoming more confrontational.

"Sorry. Usually when people ask what's wrong with me they are asking about my implant. I'm sorry for waking you," said Rian. "I'll be quiet."

Sandra gave Rian a peculiar stare, not sure what to make of this girl across from her. Her eyes moved to the implant. Rian's eyes moved to

Sandra's arm. After a moment, each girl realized that they were staring at the other and pulled their eyes away.

"Just be quiet," said Sandra, placing her head back into her arms.

After taking a few bites of her Salisbury steak and eating her cornbread, Rian pushed her tray away to make room for her sketch pad. Drawing was Rian's escape. When she created a picture, she was in charge. If she wanted a tree in the front yard, she drew a tree. If she wanted a character to have a handlebar mustache, all she had to do was draw it on the upper lip and curl it up at the ends. It was all her call.

She opened the sketch pad to an unfinished drawing of a unicorn. The mythical creature was standing on its hind legs with its horn pointed toward the sky. She put her pencil to paper and continued working on its mane. She wanted it to look as though it were blowing in the wind. Eraser marks darkened the area around the unicorn's head. She couldn't seem to get it quite right.

Rian was so focused on the drawing, she didn't notice that Luis had gotten up and was standing behind her. He held something in his hand. It was small and flat and when she wasn't paying attention, he gently stuck it to the back of her head, behind her right ear.

It was a magnet. The magnet looked like a dollop of soft serve chocolate ice cream, with no cone. It had a face made of two cartoon eyes and a big white smile. It was a poop emoji magnet. She didn't notice Luis put it there, but some of the kids around her did.

Luis covered his mouth as he backed away from her. Hassan and Wayne roared with laughter.

Shut up, he signed to them, bringing his hand to his mouth abruptly.

The boys' laughter caught Rian's attention. As she turned toward them they turned away. Luis returned to his seat and punched Hassan in the arm for drawing attention to his prank. Rian sensed that she was the brunt of a joke, but she had no idea what the joke was, and she didn't really care. She was much more interested in her unicorn.

After a few minutes, other students noticed the magnet attached to the back of her head. As they passed they too laughed out loud, raising Rian's suspicion about what Luis had done.

She turned to check her back. There was no kick me sign taped to her shirt, but the more she looked around, the more attention she drew to the magnet stuck to the back of her head.

Now the kids at the main table were laughing too, including Elisha and Jamilah. It was now clear that she was the brunt of a joke, but she had no idea what that joke was.

She looked over at Luis and asked, "What's so funny?"

Luis wrapped his left hand around the thumb on his right hand and pulled the thumb out, signing his response. She didn't understand. Then he crashed the tips of his fingers to his temple and his cheek.

Too upset to address it directly, Rian turned once again to her sketch pad and her drawing. She felt the other kids' eyes on her. Staring at her. Laughing at her. The laughter was so loud, it stirred Sandra awake once again.

She looked around, just as confused as Rian as to why everyone was laughing.

"What are they laughing at?" she asked.

"Not sure. Me, I think," Rian said nervously.

Sandra noticed that as people passed, they stared and pointed at the back of Rian's head. Some kids even got up to get a closer look. Rian was trying hard not to notice, but Sandra wanted an answer. She stood up and walked over to Rian to investigate.

When she saw the magnet stuck to Rian's head she did not laugh. She took it off and slammed it on the lunch table in front of Rian.

"This is what they're laughing at. Who put this on you?" Sandra asked.

Rian looked at Luis. So did Sandra. His demeanor changed when he saw the look on Sandra's face.

"You?" she asked Luis.

Luis stood up and signed, *Tease*.

Translating for Luis, Hassan told Sandra, "Just a joke."

"You think this is funny?" Sandra said, tossing the magnet at Luis.

He stepped toward her, and she shoved him back, returning him to his seat. Now everyone's attention was on Luis who looked as though he was seconds away from getting beat up by a one-armed girl.

"You want to see something funny?" Sandra said, grabbing Luis's half-finished carton of milk. She held it over his head. Without protest, he allowed her to pour the contents all over all over him.

The creamy brown liquid coated his face and soaked into his shirt. Luis just sat there, mortified. When she was done she tossed the empty carton on his tray.

"Yeah, that's funny too," she said.

Miss Karen, an aide, stood over Sandra with her arms folded. "Alright, let's go. I guess you enjoy eating lunch in Mr. Tasker's office."

Miss Karen took pleasure in punishing Sandra, which was a fairly regular occurrence. Sandra didn't argue. She just picked up her belongings and followed Miss Karen out the cafetorium. She never once looked back to a stunned and grateful Rian.

10

INJURY

The time-honored tradition of allowing designated captains the distinction of choosing their team was almost complete. Antoine Kennedy and Nathan Powers were chosen as team captains for boys' basketball. Mr. Bergentregger, the gym teacher, always chose Antoine and Nathan as team captains, regardless of the sport.

It's not as though they weren't deserving. They were the two most athletic boys in the sixth grade. Antoine was the fastest kid in the school. He could run a 100-meter dash in 13 seconds.

Nathan's athletic prowess was the envy of the other boys. When they played football, he was the quarterback. In baseball, he was always the best pitcher and the best hitter. Both boys dominated in basketball too. They were Mr. Burgentregger's pride and joy and the standard by which he held all other sixth-graders.

Of the twelve boys in the class that day, only two remained unchosen. Lucas, the smallest boy in the class and most likely to sit out due to injury and Shack.

The only thing Shack hated more than gym class was being chosen last in gym class. He usually just stood in the way of the other kids trying to get by him, which was a useful skill in basketball. He also didn't mind knocking people over, which was normally good enough for him to be chosen somewhere in the middle of the pack.

"Luke," Antoine called out, pointing to Lucas.

Surprised, Lucas smiled and looked over at Shack. A big mistake. Shack snarled back, causing Lucas's smile to evaporate as he ran to Mr. Bergentregger to collect his orange pinny.

Nathan turned his back to Shack and headed toward center court. Bergentregger motioned for Shack to join his team.

Nathan and Antoine were conspiring against him. During recess, Shack ended their game of kickball early, launching the bouncy red sphere over the recess yard fence by kicking it with his size twelve sneaker. He was upset after a disagreement about whether or not he was tagged out had not been decided his way.

The recess aides did not allow anyone to climb the fence to get a ball and shortly thereafter recess ended, as did the game. Which ended in a tie.

Luis was playing on Antoine's team. He was Antoine's first pick. He had excellent ball control skills, was a tremendous passer, and was one of the only kids who could actually put the ball in the basket.

For the past two weeks, Antoine and Luis had played as teammates in the Northeast Philadelphia Junior Basketball League. With basketball, it didn't matter that Luis and Antoine couldn't speak to one another. They could communicate with a look, a shift, or a raised hand. When Luis played basketball, he felt and was treated like everyone else in the class. In fact, he was treated better, because his game had to be respected.

The game started with Antoine's team jumping out to a big lead. Luis was undoubtedly the third best basketball player in the class, which made the matchup more of a 2 on 1 affair. Nathan would take the ball down the court and shoot a layup or a shot in the paint, then Antoine or Luis would get a rebound and pass the ball the other way and score.

Nathan had to be perfect, because he couldn't guard Antoine and Luis at the same time. The rest of the boys served mainly as on-court spectators, trying to stay out of the way.

Shack stood in the center of the court and refused to move. Once Mr. Burgentregger whistled for him to "shake a leg," so Shack slowly stepped to one side of the court until the action shifted to the other side. Burgentregger acknowledged the uselessness of trying to get Shack to move, so he stopped trying.

At one point in the game, Reg Mosely managed to get his hand in and knock the ball loose from Antoine. The ball bounced behind everyone and rolled directly to Shack, a statue in the center of the court. He reached down and picked it up.

Nathan and the others ran to him and signaled for him to pass. Shack stood for a moment and taunted the other boys, pretending to pass it. Nathan got away from Luis, who was covering him, giving Shack a clear shot to get him the ball. Again, Shack faked it his way, then pulled it back.

"Come on, Shack. Pass it!" Nathan yelled.

Shack tucked the ball under his arm and against his waist and stood stupidly admiring the others around him. Mr. Burgentregger was about to blow the whistle, when Luis reached behind him and punched the ball loose. Shack, more interested in punching back than the game, turned to see who stole the ball and tripped over his own foot. He came crashing to the floor at the same time Luis bounded in front of him.

With a head of steam, Luis ran down the court and shot an easy layup. Antoine high-fived Luis. Running back to the other end of the court, Luis and Antoine laughed at Shack as he sat sprawled out in the center of the floor.

The game continued for another ten minutes, with Antoine and Luis's team pulling away. After the humiliating steal, Shack returned to his post in the center of the court, where he stood like a sentry.

Nathan hit a three-pointer, and Antoine grabbed the ball. He passed it to Luis, who darted around Reg Mosley like a car zigzagging through traffic.

Shack finally left center court and backpedaled his way to the hoop. Standing directly under the basket, he was the only person between Luis and another easy layup. Luis headed straight for him.

Within striking distance, Luis left his feet and rolled the ball off his fingertips. As if drawn to the basket, the shot rolled in with ease. Luis pivoted and started to run back toward the other end of the court.

Before he could take three steps, Shack kicked out his right foot and caught Luis's left. He didn't just put his foot in the way, he literally kicked his massive trunk-sized calf out and hit Luis squarely in the ankle. Both fell to the floor, Shack acted as though the collision was a mistake.

Luis grabbed his ankle and hollered in pain. He rolled on the court, clutching the quickly swelling joint.

Mr. Burgentregger blew his whistle and ran onto the court.

"Hold up. We have a man down," he said.

Mr. Rose, sitting on a folding chair the whole time reading a book, got up to interpret for the teacher.

"Let me see that ankle," said Mr. Burgentregger.

Luis released his grip and showed it to his teacher. It was badly swollen. Luis gnashed his teeth to cope with the pain.

"I'm hurt, too," Shack said, rubbing the side of his thigh.

Mr. Burgentregger turned angrily to Shack and said, "That didn't look like a mistake to me."

"It wasn't. He didn't look where he was going. He ran right into me," said Shack. "Can I go to the nurse or what?"

"We better get you both to the nurse," Burgentregger said, rising to his feet.

He considered punishing Shack but knew he couldn't prove that he'd meant to do it. He believed it, but he couldn't prove it. Besides, that kind of accusation required the principal to investigate, and a report to be written. It might even lead to a conference with parents, and Burgentregger wasn't interested in all of that.

"Come on, someone help me get these two to the nurse," he said.

11

PARTNERS

The next day in Mr. Herman's Math class, when it was once again time to partner up, Rian was relieved to see that Hector had returned. Wayne could go back to copying his work, and Rian could go back to working by herself. The way she liked it. Mr. Herman had other plans for Rian however.

"Rain, you're going to work with Sandra today," he said startling both girls.

Sandra and Rian looked at each other. Suddenly the idea of working with Sandra made Rian nervous. She wasn't nervous when she asked Sandra to work with her on the state project, but now she felt uneasy.

Why did Sandra come to her defense the other day? What was her deal? Rian wondered. The unpredictability of her personality put Rian on edge.

Rian got up, grabbed her math journal and headed over to Sandra's desk. Sandra was back to counting the holes in the ceiling tiles. Rian turned the empty desk around to face Sandra. She wasn't going to make the same mistake she made with Elisha.

"Hi," said Rian in a small squeaky voice.

Sandra did not respond, her head remained tilted back, and her eyes remained on the ceiling. Rian opened her journal to page 49 and saw that the first question asked her to calculate the circumference of a circle using Pi.

"Hey, why won't the other numbers talk to Pi at parties?" she asked Sandra excitedly.

Tilting her head down to finally acknowledge Rian, Sandra asked, "What?"

It's a Pi joke. Why won't the other numbers talk to Pi at parties?" she repeated.

She waited for Sandra to ask why for an uncomfortably long time. Giving up, Rian said, "Because he just goes on and on and on." Delighted with her joke, Rian chuckled.

Sandra was not amused. "You're corny," she said, returning her head to the familiar position of looking skyward.

"Yeah, I guess I am pretty corny." Rian's agreement with Sandra's insult garnered another crooked look from her reluctant partner.

Sandra's refusal to speak made Rian even more uneasy. This had the effect of making Rian talk even more, just to break the uncomfortable silence between them.

"Do you live in this neighborhood? I'm on Millbrook Drive. I used to live in Penn Hills. I am still trying to get used to Philly. Have you always lived in…."

"Enough with you," Sandra barked at Rian.

"Sorry, I just thought…" Rian was cut off by an irate Sandra.

"Did you hear me? Shut up."

"I heard you. I'm not deaf. I have this hearing loss. It's not a problem, it's just, you know, I don't hear like the other kids in this school."

"Yeah, well you're lucky. I hate this place. I wish I didn't have to hear these people," said Sandra. "They're loud. I like the quiet."

"Okay," Rian sprang up from her seat. "I can fix that."

Confused, Sandra watched as Rian walked to Mr. Herman's desk. There was a brief exchange between them, and after a moment of making her case, Mr. Herman nodded his head, conceding something. Rian walked back to Sandra's desk and grabbed her Math journal.

"Come on, let's get away from all this noise. We're going to work in the hall," she said.

Sandra wasn't at all interested in finding the circumference of a circle, but the opportunity to get out of Mr. Herman's class was too good an offer to pass up. Leaving her Math journal comfortably tucked in the far recesses of her desk, Sandra got up and followed Rian out of the class.

She found Rian sitting against the wall. Rian smiled at Sandra as she slowly walked over. She turned, pressed her back to the wall and slid into a seated position next to Rian.

"What did you say to him?" she asked Rian.

"That I wanted to work out here. It's hard sometimes for me to hear my partner when everyone else is talking. He said no at first, but my IEP allows me to do it."

"I'm going to tell my mom to put that in my IEP. I hate being around them. All of them," said Sandra.

"I'm starting to feel the same way," said Rian.

"They're corny. All of them. I miss my old school," she said.

"Me too," said Rian. "Everyone in this school is so mean."

"And corny," said Sandra.

"Why did you help me the other day? I mean, everyone else thought Luis's joke was funny, but you didn't. I appreciate what you did, but why did you do it?" Rian asked.

"I don't know. Just made me mad. Like, you weren't bothering nobody. Why do they want to bother you? I didn't think about it, I just did it." Sandra replied.

"Did you get in trouble?" Rian asked.

"No. They can't really do anything to me here, 'cause I don't care enough for anything they do to matter. My sped teacher's making me eat lunch with her this week," said Sandra.

"Did you tell her what happened? That seems unfair, I mean, they're always telling us to stand up to bullies. Be a friend. That was all you did…"

"I ain't a snitch," Sandra interrupted. "Like I said, they can't do anything to me. I don't have to eat with those clowns. I'm good."

"Well, thank you," said Rian.

Rian pulled her book closer and started working on the first problem. She noticed right away that Sandra didn't have her book.

"So how come you talk so good?" asked Sandra.

"What do you mean?" asked Rian.

"Hassan talks funny. Luis don't talk at all. I thought you were deaf?" Sandra asked. "If you're deaf, why don't you talk like them?"

"It's complicated," said Rian. She closed her book and readied herself for her prepared response to the question.

"I have these implants," Rian pointed to her right side, forgetting there was not an implant there, thanks to Shack. "I can hear most everything a deaf person can't hear."

"So you're not deaf?" Sandra asked.

"I am. I used to be like them. I had some hearing, like Wayne and Hassan. They talk differently because that's how they hear everyone else speak. When I got my second implant, I lost all my residual hearing. So if this isn't on my head, I can't hear anything."

"That's funny," said Sandra.

"What's funny?" asked Rian.

"What you said, residual hearing. My doctor calls this my residual limb," Sandra said, holding up her arm. "Most people call it a stump. I hate that. Like it's a tree someone cut down. It ain't a stump."

"Yeah, people always say I'm deaf. I like to be called hearing impaired." Rian said.

"You like to be called hearing impaired? That sounds worse than deaf," exclaimed Sandra.

"Really? I don't know, my Hearing teacher in my other school always said I should tell people I'm hearing impaired."

"You know why I poured that milk on Luis. You are the only person in this school that talked to me and didn't ask about my arm. I hate that. People always want to ask me about it. Like, there's nothing else about me to talk about."

"I know," Rian sat up excitedly. "People always ask about my implants. They're just a tool. They're not me. I hate it."

"You're not deaf, and you're not hearing impaired. You're Rain," said Sandra.

"No, I'm Rian. Mr. Herman calls me Rain because he can't read."

They laughed.

"Yeah, he's corny too!" said Sandra.

Rian and Sandra spent the rest of the period talking about everything except Math. For the first time since starting at Hancock, Rian felt as though she'd finally made a friend.

12

REMOTE CONTROL

Rian sat in the front row, on the far right side of the computer lab. She was assigned a seat between Hassan and Luis. She felt it was unfair that all the other students were allowed to choose their own seats, while she as always, had to be assigned to a seat in the front of the room.

Everyone else got to sit next to a friend. Over the past few weeks Rian and Sandra had become very friendly. She wanted to sit next to her in the back of the room far away from Hassan and Luis. She tried to convince Miss Hughes that being singled out because of her hearing loss violated her civil rights. Miss Hughes did not agree.

The class was busy creating PowerPoint slides for an American Revolution project. After the laptop debacle, Mrs. Bae-Huley decided the lab was a better option for any computer-related work.

Mr. Rose loved the time spent in the computer lab. Normally, Social Studies meant furiously translating information about the responsibilities of the three branches of government or describing the interactions of consumers and producers in the national economy. In the lab, he sat in front of Luis, Hassan, and Wayne and read a novel.

Mrs. Bae-Huley gave some basic instruction on PowerPoint and then expected students to figure out the how to make their presentations on their own. It seemed clear to the class that she didn't know PowerPoint very well.

Rian was working on a presentation about The Battle of Bunker Hill. Thirty minutes in, she was already working on slide number eleven.

"Mrs. Bae-Huley," Lucas's voice called from the back of the lab. "How do I insert a picture into the presentation?"

"Can someone please show Lucas how to put a picture into his presentation?" Mrs. Bae-Huley asked, her voice belting out of Rian's large black FM speaker.

That hideous silver microphone hanging around Mrs. Bae-Huley's neck tethered Rian to the speaker. She hated the speaker. She turned her focus from the computer screen to the speaker and glared at it. A couple of times she tried to leave it behind or turn it off, but it never worked.

Reluctant to use it at first, it was now clear that Mrs. Bae-Huley loved the speaker. More specifically, Mrs. Bae-Huley loved the sound of her voice amplified through the speaker. For a short time, she thought it was funny to hold the microphone in her hand and sing into it. On the day she sang "Smooth Criminal," Rian pleaded with Miss Hughes to talk to Mrs. Bae-Huley and ask her to stop. Which she did, reluctantly.

No one offered to help Lucas. Timidly, he raised his hand once again. Mrs. Bae-Huley saw the hand, rolled her eyes, and got up from her seat to help.

"No, click this here…" her short-tempered direction to Lucas carried through Rian's speaker. This happened a lot. There was a mute button on the microphone, but Mrs. Bae-Huley rarely bothered with it.

Rian raised her hand and asked, "Mrs. Bae-Huley, can you please turn off the microphone?"

"Of course, Rian," she said, grabbing it and searching for the off switch. She fumbled with it. Her long fingernails beat against the top of the microphone causing an awful series of clicking and banging noises to be sent through the speaker.

"There, is that better?" she asked, her voice shot through the speaker and hit Rian in the head like rock off a slingshot.

"Yes," Rian rolled her eyes as she answered.

Discreetly, Rian turned the speaker off and just in time. From across the room, Mrs. Bae-Huley saw Hassan and Luis in an animated conversation and yelled, "Stop fooling around and get to work!"

"Continue," signed Mr. Rose, placing his book gently on his knee.

The two boys laughed, even after Mr. Rose lazily suggested they get back to work. Despite her utter hatred of these two, Rian was curious to know what was so funny.

She took a peek at Hassan's computer screen. He wasn't working on his presentation. He wasn't even using PowerPoint. Instead, his screen showed an Amazon page advertising a footbath on sale for $29.99.

Hassan saw Rian looking at his screen, tried to turn it away from her and declared, "Not your business!"

He did not mean to be so loud, but he was not always aware of just how powerful his voice could be.

The short exchange gave Mrs. Bae-Huley the excuse she was looking for to abandon Lucas, and his quest to insert an image into his presentation and turn her attention to a skill she was infinitely more comfortable using. Yelling.

"I thought I told you to get back to work!" she hollered as she stampeded toward Rian and Hassan.

Fumbling with the mouse, Hassan minimized the screen he had open and pulled his presentation back up.

"What are you two doing?" Mrs. Bae-Huley demanded.

"Hassan put a link to a website in his presentation. I was just asking how he did it."

Rian's response was a lie that surprised Hassan but not nearly as much as it surprised Rian herself. For some reason she felt compelled to keep him from getting in trouble.

"A link to a website," Mrs. Bae-Huley repeated suspiciously.

"Can you show me how to add a link to a website?" Rian asked, trying to get Mrs. Bae-Huley's attention back.

"Well, I have to help Lucas add a picture. Hassan, show Rian how to link a website."

The lie worked. Mrs. Bae-Huley wanted nothing to do with Rian's request, so she turned around and headed back to Lucas' computer.

When she was gone, Hassan turned to Rian and said, "Thanks."

Luis asked Hassan what happened, and when he explained, Luis looked at Rian confused.

Mrs. Bae-Huley returned to her desk and whatever it was she was doing on her computer. When he was sure she couldn't see their screens, Luis tapped Hassan's arm and urged him to return to the shenanigans they were enjoying before being interrupted. Checking to make sure Mrs. Bae-Huley was not watching the class, Hassan pulled up the Amazon page once again.

"I don't understand. You're buying a footbath?" Rian asked, perplexed. "I don't get it."

Feeling obligated to explain, Hassan held his hands up, not touching the mouse or the keyboard and said, "Watch."

At first nothing happened. Then suddenly Rian noticed something peculiar. Although Hassan kept his hands off the computer, the page began scrolling by itself. The cursor slid over to a blue and white *Buy Now* button at the bottom of the page, clicked it and a new page appeared. Suddenly credit card numbers appeared one at a time in a little white box followed by Mrs. Bae-Huley's name and address.

Cecil Bae-Huley. 909 Rose Ln. Philadelphia, PA.

8472 1730 4482 7253 (credit card number)

"How are you doing that?" Rian asked.

"Not me. Her," Hassan said, pointing directly at Mrs. Bae-Huley.

Rian watched as her teacher typed on the computer, then turned back to Hassan and watched as information filled the blank boxes on his screen. A moment later, click, the purchase was made.

Rian looked back at Mrs. Bae-Huley. She slipped a blue credit card into a pink leather wallet, fastened the clip and placed it in her purse.

"Does she know you can see her computer?" asked Rian.

"No. I can see all computer," said Hassan, pointing around the room. "This have a program. It was open when I sit down."

Annoyed by their conversation, Luis hit Hassan in the arm and signed, *Don't-tell her. She-will snitch.*

"What did he say?" Rian asked.

"He say you will snitch," answered Hassan.

"What does that mean?" Rian asked.

"It means you tell," replied Hassan.

Rian turned to Luis. She placed her finger over her lips, a gesture meant to communicate that she would keep her mouth shut.

After more discussion, Luis gave up, and Hassan continued. He clicked a tab, and a list of computers in the room appeared on his screen. It was a list of blue hyperlinks with numbers attached. He clicked on number 13, and a screen popped up showing someone playing a game with a miner digging tunnels in the ground.

Rian looked around. The computers had numbered cards in front of them. She looked at 13. Maurice, an African-American boy with a curved part shaved into his scalp, was hitting keys furiously.

"How do I do that?" she asked.

"Only me." Hassan smiled coyly. He pointed the card in front of his computer. It did not have a number in front of it. It had an abbreviation. It read, "Admin."

Rian chuckled as her eyes darted around the room.

"You're going to get in trouble," she said.

"No tell!" Hassan reminded her.

Annoyed, Luis hit Hassan's arm again and signed, *Translate*!

Hassan swiped his hand across his forehead and signed, *Forgot*.

He clicked through other computers on the list. Number 6 was working on the project. So were 8 and 14. Number 20 was watching a video of a cat staring at a birthday cake and 22 wasn't doing anything.

"Bae-Hue is the more fun." Hassan said clicking on number 9, her computer. She was no longer shopping. She was writing an email.

"You shouldn't look at that," Rian said, turning away. "It's private."

"It fine. She not know," he said confidently.

Hassan was right. Mrs. Bae-Huley failed to notice that she placed Hassan on the computer meant for the teacher. An honest mistake since she was told by Miss Hughes to seat them at the far end of the lab away from the air vent, which rattled furiously.

Rian couldn't take her eyes off Hassan's screen. She knew it was wrong, but it was just too tempting. The left side of his screen listed emails sitting in the teacher's inbox. On the right side, words appeared to write themselves. Rian's eyes darted from Hassan's screen to Mrs. Bae-Huley, who typed away on the keyboard.

Her ability to type was impressively fast. So fast that whole words appeared on Hassan's screen. The email she wrote was addressed to ALL STAFF, and the subject line read Highways.

Friends,

Has anyone seen my copy of the 6th grade _Highways_ Teacher's Edition English textbook? It's been missing since Monday. It may have been left by the copier in the lounge. If you see it, please return it or let me know so I can retrieve it asap!

- Cil

After typing her name, the cursor moved to the top left of the screen, and she clicked an icon that looked like a paper airplane. The email was sent with an accompanying sound of a plane taking off that Hassan was unable to hear.

The sound came from both computers, drawing Mrs. Bae-Huley's attention. She lifted her head up and gave a curious glance around the room. Although Hassan and Luis were oblivious, Rian heard it. She tapped Hassan and pointed toward Mrs. Bae-Huley.

"Close it," she whispered to him.

"What?" he asked her loudly.

Rian pointed to her ear and nodded her head in Mrs. Bae-Huley's direction. Finally catching on, Hassan pressed the X in the top right corner of his screen, and the email account was gone.

13

CITALDI'S

Luis spent the morning in physical therapy working out the injury to his ankle. It was healing but not fast enough. He was told he couldn't play basketball for at least a month, if not longer. Doing the math, Luis knew that meant his basketball season was over.

As if he wasn't in a bad enough mood already, after the appointment Jennifer brought him to the Franklin Mills Mall to buy cold weather clothes for his baby brother. He didn't mind the mall, but he had no interest in spending his afternoon in Sophistikids or The Children's Place.

Luis lagged behind as Jennifer pushed a stroller along a black-and-white tile floor that looked like a sprawling chessboard with no end in sight. A two-dimensional disembodied head of Benjamin Franklin hovered over mall-goers like Big Brother, urging patrons to "Shop or Die". Just beyond Mr. Franklin's watchful eye was Luis's favorite store, Foot Locker.

Luis quickened his pace and pulled on Jennifer's shirt. She stopped the stroller, knowing what he was about to ask and turned to look at him anyway.

I-want to-shop-there, he signed.

Jennifer made a swift chop gesture by her neck, indicating she was *broke*, and did not have money for shoes.

Luis went into meltdown mode. He tried to stomp his feet, but the moment he slammed his walking boot onto the tiled floor, a pain shot into his ankle, ending that tantrum and sending him into another. He wailed loudly, clutching the joint and collapsing to the floor below.

Jennifer's expression morphed from frustration to rage. With both hands on the stroller she charged toward him, ready to end this embarrassing display.

Recognizing her look, Luis pulled himself up. Jennifer stopped, turned around, and continued walking toward Sophistikids. He lumbered behind, dragging his injured leg and moaning loudly, giving mall shoppers reason to stare. Luis fell farther and farther behind his mother with his childish behavior.

Jennifer stopped outside of Sophistikids with her arms folded and waited for her son. In the distance between the store and Luis was a pretzel stand with the name Citaldi's emblazoned in green letters embossed with black outlines. Citaldi's Pretzels was an institution in Northeast Philadelphia. The stand in the mall was the newest of the many franchises around that part of the city. The tremendously long line stretched past three different stores.

Luis stopped altogether as he excitedly pointed to the stand and signed, *Pretzels!*

Jennifer's impatient expression remained unchanged as she waited for him to join her. Realizing she wasn't going to allow this either, Luis dropped his head and continued his walking toward his mother, defeated. His pace was slower and even more plodding as he passed Citaldi's customers one after the next. As he dragged himself toward her, he saw a familiar face. It was Rian.

Aunt Nancy had invited Rian to join her for some shopping earlier that morning. Unlike Joanna, Nancy had no problem what-so-ever allowing Rian the freedom to explore Franklin Mills on her own as long as Rian kept quiet about it. She, like Luis, saw Citaldi's and decided she had to have a pretzel. Unlike Jennifer, Nancy agreed.

Luis was surprised to see Rian. She saw him too, but so did everyone else in the line. He was really making a scene, and there was not much else to entertain the people waiting to place their order. For a moment Luis and Rian caught each other's gaze. Rian turned her head, not wanting Luis to know that she saw him. Surprisingly, he raised his hand and waved to her.

The wave caught Rian off guard. *Should I wave back,* she thought to herself. *Why is he waving to me?*

She felt obligated to wave back. She looked around to see if he was actually waving at someone else, but he continued waving and staring right at her, and now it was clear that she saw the gesture.

Limply, Rian waved back.

Luis finally reached Jennifer, who turned to enter the store. He grabbed her shirt again and tugged hard.

Please, he begged with a pathetic expression on his face.

I-don't want you-in line-alone, she signed.

I'm not-alone. My-friend-is there! The lie surprised him, even as he pointed at Rian.

Luis threw his hands in the air and waved them frantically over his head. He called out to Rian to get her attention. The primal sound echoed off the walls, glass ceiling, and tile floors of the mall, startling all the hearing people within earshot.

Rian heard him too and looked his way. She saw Luis waving his arms again. Once again he waved to her and smiled. Still confused, she smiled and waved back.

It was a risk. From where Jennifer stood, she was unlikely to notice that Rian wore a cochlear implant. He wanted that pretzel. He needed that pretzel and so in that moment he gambled that she would not see Rian's implant.

Luis turned to Jennifer and signed, *She's-my-friend-from-school.*

Her-name? Jennifer asked, throwing her hands on her hips and looking at her son suspiciously.

With his fingers crossed, Luis reached behind his ear but stopped in mid-motion. He knew he couldn't tap the back of his head behind his ear with the name sign he'd given Rian. That would make it totally obvious that she had an implant. Thinking quickly, Luis gave her a new name sign, twirling an *R* from his ear to his shoulder to emphasize her long red ringlets of hair.

Rian watched the conversation between Luis and Jennifer, fascinated. She was starting to love sign language, and she wished she knew it.

Worn down, Jennifer reached into her purse and pulled out a five-dollar bill. He snatched it before she could reconsider and headed directly toward Rian.

She stood in the middle of the line. Luis walked up and stood beside her. She found this action to be brazen. She hated when people cut in line. She was sure it must have upset the people behind her.

I didn't invite him to stand with me. To cut in line. Who does he think he is? Rian wondered to herself.

Luis turned to Rian and flashed the letters *O-K* to her for approval.

Because she was a pushover, Rian smiled and said, "Okay."

Luis looked back at Jennifer, who watched her son carefully.

Continuing the charade, Luis flicked his wrist pulling his fingers up off his chest and asked, *What's up?*

Rian didn't understand. She just smiled and nodded in agreement. Luis rolled his eyes and shook his head no, keeping one eye on his mother. He repeated the motion slower this time, and he tried to say the words more clearly.

This time she understood. Rian shook her head back and forth, hoping he would understand that she meant to say, "Nothing."

Satisfied Luis was with a friend, Jennifer pushed the stroller and disappeared into Sophistikids. When she was gone Luis no longer seemed interested in talking to Rian.

They stood for a few minutes not looking at one another, but then a thought came to Luis. He liked Sandra a lot. He noticed that recently she and Rian were eating together, partnering in class and even hanging out during recess. Since Rian was, at least in that moment, acting friendly toward Luis, maybe he could get to know Sandra better by pretending to like Rian.

He turned back to her. Raising his hand to his face, Luis made a sign as if he were pretending to put something in his mouth. Rian knew what he was trying to say! He wanted to know what she was going to eat. Without knowing how to sign a response, Rian over- exaggerated the words "cinn-a-mon twistssss."

Luis laughed at the way she said the words, but he understood. He repeated her words using his broken speech, "cinnamon twists."

Then, Luis put his clenched fist to his mouth and kissed it signing, *I- love them*!

She had no idea what he meant, but his face suggested he liked cinnamon twists too. She tried to ask Luis what he wanted to eat. She pointed at him and copied his sign, *Eat?*

Bugs, he signed, putting his thumb to the end of his nose and wiggling his fingers.

Rian was lost. Instead of admitting she didn't understand his answer, she nodded her head and smiled a large toothy grin. She held up her fist and kissed it, suggesting she too loved to eat bugs.

Luis fell over laughing. He laughed so hard and loud that the people around them turned to stare. Rian knew right away that he was laughing at her. She turned away from him and faced forward.

Why was she even trying? Luis had been nothing but cruel to her up until now. Clearly, whatever this was, it wasn't him trying to be friends.

Luis felt a small twinge of guilt. He didn't like Rian, but she was willing to help him get into that line, so he stopped laughing. He tapped her shoulder to get her attention, but she turned her head, her body stiff, and faced forward. He rolled a closed fist around his chest and signed, *Sorry*.

She recognized that sign too. When Rian was very young, Joanna tried to teach Rian sign language. It didn't last, and she hadn't learned much, but she did remember a few signs.

She signed *sorry* once after she broke her father's camera lens. She knocked it off his desk by mistake; while building a Lego ice cream shop she bumped the camera with her arm and watched as the lens rolled and fell off the table and onto the floor. She was so upset she couldn't talk through her tears. She signed the word *sorry* instead.

Giving in once again, she nodded to Luis and fingerspelled, *O-K.*

A quick inventory of all the signs Rian learned when she was little made for a very short list: happy, hungry, please, finish, sorry, sign, mom, dad, and monkey (she had been a big fan of a show with a cartoon monkey when she was very little). Those were the only signs that she remembered.

You know-sign language? Luis asked suspiciously.

The expression on his face was enough for her to understand his question. She showed Luis all the signs she knew. She ended by turning out her open palms and signed, *Finished.*

They smiled at one another, surprised at the pleasant interaction they were engaged in and then stood together in silence until they got to the front of the line.

"Welcome to Citaldi's, where the pretzels are primo," said a woman behind the counter in a deep manly voice. The kind of raspy tone born out of years of smoking a pack of cigarettes every day.

"Cinnamon twists," said Rian.

"Size?" the woman asked.

"Medium," Rian replied.

"What about you?" she asked, turning her attention to Luis.

Luis reached into his pocket to grab his cellphone out of habit. Normally, he used a texting app to communicate with hearing people. Plunging his hands deep into his pocket, he remembered the phone had gone missing earlier in the week. Without it, ordering his pretzel was going to be a challenge.

Luis pinched his index finger and thumb together and pretended to scribble across his left hand in an attempt to ask the woman for a pencil.

"What is he doing?" she asked.

"I'm not sure. I think he wants you to give him a pencil," Rian replied.

"What for? Can't he talk?" the woman asked.

"No, he's deaf," Rian said.

"Fantastic," the woman replied, turning her head away and scanning the area for a pencil. After a half-hearted, ten-second search, she brought her attention back to Rian.

"Nope, no pencil. Just tell me what he wants?"

Rian turned to Luis who knew she didn't have a pencil.

He wiggled his fingers in a way that made Rian think he was playing an imaginary piano so he could ask her to Luis asked her to, *Fingerspell-for-me*?

She didn't understand his question, so she shrugged her shoulders. Luis reconsidered how to make his request. He started signing the alphabet. By the time he reached the letter *H*, Rian understood. She smiled and nodded excitedly. She did know the alphabet, or most of it anyway.

Rian shook her head and said, "Slow."

Luis fingerspelled a word in less time than it took Rian to blink. She waved her hands in front of him with her eyes wide. Luis realized he needed to slow down.

"You're holding up the line," the woman interrupted. "Let's go."

"Please, give me a minute, I don't know sign," Rian said apologetically.

"Aren't you deaf?" the woman asked.

"No!" She replied emphatically.

"Sorry, I figured that hearing aid behind your ear..." the woman's question trailed off.

"It's not a hearing aid," she shot back annoyed. "It's an implant."

The woman looked confused, and Rian felt annoyed. She stopped trying to explain and turned back to Luis and repeated her request, "Slowly."

Luis finger spelled, *J-A-L-A-P-E-N-O*. Rian looked puzzled and shook her head.

"Sweetheart…," the pretzel woman was quickly cut off.

"I need to make sure," Rian insisted, and turned back to Luis.

She held up one finger to ask him to fingerspell the order one more time.

Luis once again signed *J-A-L-A-P-E-N-O*. Rian nodded, recognizing all the letters the second time.

"Jala peno," she said.

The woman rolled her eyes and turned to get their order. She returned with three long braided pretzel rods coated in golden cinnamon dust and a pretzel the size of a Frisbee covered in green peppers. Jalapeno peppers.

"Four-seventy five," the woman said, ringing up the sale.

Rian looked at Luis, not sure how to split the bill. Luis placed the five-dollar bill his mother gave him on the counter and smiled at Rian.

"Thanks," Rian signed, slapping her right hand from her chin into her open left palm.

A few minutes later they were sitting on a bench enjoying their prized Citaldi's pretzels. If it were a race to eat it the fastest, Luis would have won by a country mile. He practically inhaled the hot, doughy delight.

When Rian was finished she tried to sign, *thank you* by bringing her right hand from her chin to her left palm.

Luis pointed at her and copied her sign, negating her attempt by shaking his head back and forth. He repeated her sign again slowly and uttered a sound that almost sounded like a word.

81

"Goo-" he said with his voice.

Rian figured he was trying to correct her, but she didn't know what he was trying to say. She didn't nod stupidly this time though; instead she looked at him with a puzzled look on her face and gestured with a shrug that she didn't understand.

Luis dropped his hands and thought for a moment. He repeated the same motion a third time. Then he held up his thumb, using the universally understood sign for "way to go!"

She got it! She meant to sign thank you, but she signed good instead. Facial expression, context, and body language all seemed to be really good clues to figure out what Luis was saying. Communicating with Luis was not easy, but she felt she was learning.

The conversation ended abruptly when Jennifer came out of Sophistikids and walked toward them. Luis saw her coming and briskly stood at attention. His open hand moved from his chest to his chin and he signed, *My-mom.*

As she came closer a look of concern ran across her face. Recognizing he was about to get into trouble, Luis hurried over to her. Rian waved to Jennifer, but the gesture was ignored. She turned to Luis with a look of anger and signed, *Friend?*

Then she touched the back of her head with her two bent fingers.

Rian now understood the sign she saw Luis use the day they met was not just a sign for cochlear implant. It was a bad sign. For the Deaf, it was an insult. She watched as Jennifer took Luis's arm and pulled him away. Luis never looked back.

14

NAME SIGNS

The rain started early in the morning and continued all the way through lunch. Rain meant indoor recess. Rian liked indoor recess. Since destroying her implant, Shack had not so much as spoken to Rian, but recently she noticed him watching her when he thought she wasn't looking. That made her uneasy.

Although he stayed away from her, Shack still tormented other students. He repeatedly helped himself to items off Lucas's lunch tray, hurled slurs at Jamilah Massulah and gave Reg Mosley a black eye in a fight off school grounds.

Mr. Tasker had warned Shack not to bother Rian ever again, and after a weeklong suspension for breaking her implant, the warning seemed to work.   She knew, however, it was only a matter of time before he sought revenge.

With recess in the classroom, there was no way for Shack to do anything to her. Mrs. Bae-Huley was close at hand. Currently, Shack sat at his desk and played a game on a tablet, directing digital lemmings off a cliff.

Indoor recess was a loud, chaotic affair. Instead of enjoying fifteen minutes of peace, teachers had to stay in their classroom with their students, as the kids blew off a little steam. Some teachers resented the loss of those fifteen minutes. They only managed behavior that was borderline dangerous, anything else was of little concern. This was Mrs. Bae-Huley's modus operandi. Unless death was imminent, she stayed behind her desk and played on her phone, allowing students to do their thing.

The classroom was raucous. Students played board games and video games. They talked, they laughed, they cried. Lucas stood at Mrs. Bae-Huley's desk describing his Rubik's Cube. He brought it to school specifically to play with it at recess, but now it was gone. Mrs. Bae-Huley knew what a Rubik's Cube looked like, but she wasn't listening, which allowed Lucas to describe it in detail.

"It's a cube. That's why it's called Rubik's Cube. I think someone named Rubik invented it. Not sure if that's his first name or last name. Anyway, it has nine colored squares on each of its six faces, and you try to get all the same colors together." Lucas explained, proud of his use of the word *'face'* in his description, a reference to yesterday's Math lesson. Mrs. Bae-Huley nodded, never once looking up from her phone.

For most people, this was an impossible environment to sit and read in, but not for Rian. She simply popped her left implant off the back of her head and put the world on mute. She considered this the one advantages having no hearing.

A few years back, on a trip to Washington, DC, with her mom and dad, she stayed in a hotel room across the hall from a room full of rowdy college kids. They were up until three in the morning, playing music, laughing, and breaking anything that wasn't secured to the wall. Mom and Dad didn't get a minute of sleep that night. Rian, however, slept like a baby.

Ready for a break, Rian slipped a Post-it note on the last page she read and closed the book. She headed over to Sandra's desk to see what she was doing. Sandra sat at her desk in the back of the class watching videos on a tablet. Seeing Rian, she turned her attention to her new friend.

"What are you doing?" Rian asked.

"Nothing. I'm hungry," Sandra replied. "That lunch was nasty."

The day's entree was a soupy concoction of macaroni and something resembling ground beef, floating in a red puddle of liquid. It was unclear whether the red substance was broth or tomato sauce. It was a meal the students affectionately called, Barfaroni.

"I got some candy in my backpack," Rian said. Her offer propelled Sandra to her feet.

84

"Let's get it!" Sandra said excitedly.

The girls entered the coatroom where Rian's backpack hung on an old brass hook secured to the cinderblock wall. The space was a small area of the classroom designated specifically for students' coats and bags.

Two short walls formed a right angle that separated the space from the rest of the classroom. The opening on either side of the L-shaped walls served as an entrance and exit to the coatroom. Coming in the exit or out the entrance would send Mrs. Bae-Huley into a murderous rage, so you were always careful to mind your way.

Rounding the corner to enter the coatroom, Rian didn't see Luis, Hassan, and Wayne sitting on the floor by the entrance playing cards. Her foot accidentally kicked Hassan's foot, and she fell forward.

"Careful!" said Hassan.

"Sorry," she replied, righting herself.

"You be careful!" Sandra demanded in her usual confrontational tone.

Hassan looked over to Luis, who was excited to see Sandra.

Luis touched his finger to his chin and pointed it toward Sandra, then rolled his fist in a circle in the center of his chest.

Following Luis's command, Hassan apologized to Rian.

"Yeah, you are sorry," Sandra insisted.

Rian found her backpack on the floor. It had been opened, and the contents dumped out of it. Her books, the case for her implants, a small umbrella, and her sketch pad were scattered around the coatroom.

"Yo, someone trashed your stuff," Sandra said, pointing out the obvious. Turning back to the boys, she prepared an interrogation of them. "Was this you?" she demanded.

Hassan and Luis shook their heads no with wide eyes and mouths open. They did not want to be in Sandra's crosshairs.

Rian grabbed her sketch pad, which lay face down on the floor. When she turned it around she saw the picture of her unicorn had been defaced. It had horns and an arrow drawn through its head. The eyes were erased and replaced with poorly scribbled orbs meant to make it look cross-eyed. A burly mustache sprouted from its muzzle.

Rian knew who was responsible. It was Shack. She was sure of it.

"Ya'll about to get a beat down," Sandra threatened as she stepped toward the boys.

"It's no big deal," said Rian.

The damage to the picture was done with blue ink so Rian couldn't erase the marks. She picked her sketch pad off the floor and paged through it. Shack had torn some of her pictures out of the book. A landscape from a vacation in the Poconos, a still life of an avocado, and a self-portrait were all missing from the book, leaving behind perforated slivers of paper buried behind the thin metal spiral binding. Hastily, she snatched the picture and tried to hide it behind her back.

"Let me see that," Sandra said, trying to reach around to see the picture.

"It's just an old drawing," Rian said, shielding the picture from Sandra.

Despite her best effort, Sandra got hold of it. She studied the picture for a moment before handing it back to Rian.

"We gonna find out who did this," said Sandra. "Then, we gonna make them pay!"

Luis pulled himself to his feet and walked over to the girls.

"This better not be you," Sandra warned Luis, putting her finger in his chest and poking him as she spoke.

Luis just shook his head, his eyes wide and said, "Ack," doing his best to say Shack's name.

Hearing Luis speak startled them. Sandra had never heard him use his voice before. Luis waved Hassan over to help explain. Through Hassan, he told the girls that they saw Shack leaving the coatroom just as they were sneaking in.

"He's gonna pay for this," Sandra declared.

"No, he's not. It's no big deal. My stuff is picked up, and the picture wasn't that good anyway."

Luis walked over to Rian and took a look at her belongings strewn across the floor. He shook his head and thrust his hand out in front of his body, the tips of his index finger and thumb touching, the other three digits extended.

"What's that mean?" asked Rian.

"Shack is a-hole!" Hassan said, answering for Luis.

Hearing Hassan translate *a-hole* for Luis made Sandra laugh out loud. Hearing Sandra laugh made Rian laugh.

"Yo, I didn't know deaf people used bad words! Show me how to do that."

This was the first time Sandra showed any interest in sign language. Luis stepped in and demonstrated how to sign the word.

He touched his thumb and index finger together at the tip as the other three fingers remained up and spread apart. The handshape was identical to the letter *F* in the sign language alphabet. He pushed the hand forward, as if Shack were standing in front of them and again voiced the word as best he could.

Again the girls laughed as they practiced signing the word.

"Are we playing, or what?" Wayne asked, still sitting on the floor.

"What are you guys doing in here? We're not allowed to play in the coatroom." Rian asked Wayne suspiciously.

It's better-in here, Luis signed, answering Rian's question.

Rian and Sandra agreed. The chaos on the other side of the wall was ridiculous. Here, there was a relative peace and privacy that was appealing to Rian.

"You play?" Hassan asked, signing the words for Luis's benefit.

"No girls!" Wayne insisted.

He quickly backed down when Luis turned and shot him a dirty look.

"What are you playin'?" Sandra asked, curiously.

"Jack black," said Hassan. "You know how to play?"

"You mean blackjack? We gambling?" Sandra asked.

Not understanding Sandra's question, Hassan asked, "What do you mean?"

Bet! Luis signed before she could answer, flipping his upturned palms down to the floor.

"Bet money?" Hassan asked. "No money."

"I know," Rian said excitedly. She reached into the front zipper compartment of her backpack and pulled out a large bag of peanut M&Ms. "He didn't find my M&Ms! We can use these."

They divided up the candy and played together until the end of recess. Hassan had to work extra hard to translate for Luis, who was thrilled to finally have a chance to hang out with Sandra. Even if it meant hanging out with Rian too.

It rained all week, which was welcome news for Rian. Not only because it kept Shack away, but it gave Sandra and Rian an opportunity to get to know Luis, Hassan and Wayne even better.

The five of them spent every recess period hiding in that coatroom. The boys had taken it upon themselves to teach Rian and Sandra sign language. Communication wasn't easy at first.

As always, Hassan played the role as an interpreter. A familiar job for him. Mr. Rose used to translate conversations for Luis during recess, but Luis didn't like having Mr. Rose hanging around when he was chilling with friends.

The decision to move on from using Mr. Rose during recess came to a head when Luis was in the fourth grade. As an interpreter Mr. Rose understood his responsibility was to translate messages and nothing more. He held to that principle religiously.

Shortly after Christmas break, during his fourth-grade year, Luis decided he no longer wanted Mr. Rose to translate for him. His teacher at the time, Mrs. Schiffman, insisted Luis permit Mr. Rose to "do his job!" Despite pushback from both Luis and Mr. Rose, Mrs. Schiffman demanded they stay together during recess.

Frustrated about having Mr. Rose always by his side, Luis stopped worrying about pragmatics. He knew whatever he signed would be spoken by Mr. Rose. Every so often, Mr. Rose would shoot Luis a disapproving look when he cursed, but he refused to change the message, correct Luis's behavior, or tell the teacher about it. His principles led to some very inappropriate translations between the boys in the early years, before Hassan learned to sign.

Hassan started at Hancock in the second grade, and by the middle of fourth grade, he was fluent in sign language. After a while, Luis was signing to Hassan from across the room during class.

One day, during a lesson about the American Revolution, Luis started signing with Hassan during Mrs. Schiffman's lesson about his intention to destroy his friend in NBA Live after school.

I'm gonna-beat-your-butt, Luis insisted. Though Luis chose a more colorful word than *butt* however, figuring the conversation enjoyed its usual discretion.

As a highly qualified, multi-licensed professional, Mr. Rose understood that there are two responsibilities every sign language interpreter must carry out in the classroom. The first and most obvious is to translate everything said by the teachers and students from English to ASL. The second responsibility is to translate everything signed by the Deaf student from ASL to English.

It was this latter responsibility Mr. Rose used to make his point.

Just as Mrs. Schiffman began her lesson on the Boston Tea Party, Mr. Rose called out, "I'm going to beat your butt," translating Luis's contribution to the class conversation. Despite Luis's use of a more colorful word than *butt*, Mr. Rose opted to keep it clean.

Mrs. Schiffman, startled by the outburst, stopped dead in her tracks.

"Excuse me, Mr. Rose?" she stammered as she spoke.

"I'm gonna make it rain. My mom could beat you," Mr. Rose continued, refusing to look at her.

"Mr. Rose, that's enough! My mother was a saint!" she said, changing her tone from confusion to anger. The class buzzed with laughter.

"I'm just voicing for Luis," he said, pointing in Luis's direction.

Luis didn't notice Mr. Rose voicing for him. He didn't notice everyone in class looking at him and laughing either. When he turned back to the lesson, Mr. Rose pointed two fingers from his eyes to Mrs. Schiffman. She was as red as a hydrant.

That was the last time Luis and Hassan signed to each other during a lesson. It was also the last time Mrs. Schiffman told Mr. Rose how to do his job, freeing Luis to enjoy recess without an adult by his side.

At first, Luis showed Rian and Sandra the basics. Signs for Xbox and PlayStation were followed by categories of words like lunchmeat, candy bars, and superhero movie titles. When Luis finished teaching those words it was time to move on to the really important stuff. The words Sandra continued to ask about again and again. Swear words.

Luis signed something to Hassan, and Hassan laughed.

"What's so funny?" asked Rian.

Hassan waved his hand at Rian as he tried to collect himself.

"He say something funny about me?" Sandra asked with a threatening tone.

Luis repeated the sign wrapping his left hand around his thumb. Then he pulled the thumb down and out of the grasp of his opposite hand.

Luis made the sign a third time, and the girls copied his motion. Sandra, unable to grasp her thumb, simply rested it at the end of her limb and pulled it down with a thrusting motion.

Rian dropped her thumb from the opposite hand's grasp. Hassan worked to correct Rian's form. Signing slowly with each movement intentional and exaggerated, she mimicked his motion, continuing to limply pull her thumb downward from the grasp of her right hand.

"What does it mean?" she asked.

"Pull hard, like this," Hassan said, performing the sign with a quick movement downward.

Rian repeated the sign, this time thrusting the thumb out of the opposite hand's grasp. Her performance sent Luis and Hassan into hysterics. Rian's laughter followed theirs.

"What does it mean, yo?" Sandra grew impatient with their laughter.

"Poop," said Hassan.

His words instantly reminded Rian of the day Luis put the emoji on the back of her head. Sandra laughed, but Rian did not. It remained one of the most hurtful things anyone had done to her. It struck her in that moment how quickly things had changed. After that day she never wanted to see Luis or Hassan again. Now here she was spending recess with them, learning to sign.

"He said, poop!" Sandra said laughing. "Yo, that's funny!" she leaned into Rian and gave her a gentle shove to get her to laugh. Giving in and letting go, Rian joined the others and enjoyed the moment.

Their laughter was loud enough to get Mrs. Bae-Huley to put down her cell phone, get up from her desk, and investigate the "shenanigans" as she liked to call them, coming from the coat closet.

She stormed around the corner and anchored her hands to her hips.

"I thought I told you I don't want anyone playing in the coatroom during recess. Was I not clear?"

"Sorry, Bae-Lu-Lee. We teach Rian and Sandra sign language." Whenever Hassan would say Mrs. Bae-Huley's name, it came out wrong. It wasn't his fault, her name just contained some sounds that were difficult for him to pronounce. It never stopped Mrs. Bae-Huley from trying to correct him.

"Bae-Hu-ley." She corrected him, extending the 'U' sound in an elongated, unnatural way. When she said "Huley," she said it in two parts, almost as if it were two words—"Hue. Lee"—with a hard break in between the syllables.

Hassan tried to say her name again exactly the way she said it. It came out, "Ba. Hue. EE."

Watching Hassan and Mrs. Bae-Huley practice speech was awful. Luis attempted to change the topic.

Name-sign? Luis suggested to Hassan.

Rian recognized both words, *name* and *sign*. She felt proud of herself for understanding but was confused by the meaning.

"We want to give you name sign." Hassan said to Mrs. Bae-Huley.

"A name sign?" she asked, confused.

"Yeah," Hassan said excitedly.

"What is a name sign?"

"Letters from your name, and do it like a sign."

Hassan pointed at Luis. He made an *L* handshape with his index finger and thumb and put the tip of his thumb on his temple.

"That's the sign for Luis?" she asked, straining to show interest.

"Letter *L*," Hassan said while holding up the sign for the letter *L*. "Here 'cause Lou is a boy." Hassan returned the letter *L* to his temple.

Luis banged Hassan in the arm. He repeated the letter *L* with his right hand, but instead of placing it on his forehead, he placed it in the center of his chest and drew an imaginary *S* across the front of his shirt.

"Sorry, I forget," Hassan said repeating the sign. "This is Lou's name."

"What is that?" asked Rian.

Hassan repeated the name sign. When he did the motion across his chest, he said, "This is for Superman. Lou love Superman."

Sandra rolled her eyes, unimpressed.

Now-we-want-to give you-a name-sign, Luis signed to Mrs. Bae-Huley.

"That's fine. Go ahead, give me a name sign," she responded.

Hassan looked at Luis, and Luis nodded. Luis signed the letter *B* and held it at an angle just below his face, as if it was a paper he was reading.

Speaking to Mrs. Bae-Huley, Hassan said, "B."

Mrs. Bae-Huley copied the sign but held her hand out with her fingers facing the boys. Hassan corrected her by turning her hand around.

Next, Luis signed *H* with his other hand. He stroked his index and middle fingers up and down in front of the *B* handshape as if he were painting it with long brush strokes.

"*H* for Hue-EE," Hassan said, over pronouncing each syllable.

Again, Mrs. Bae-Huley repeated the motion for her name sign.

Luis and Hassan cracked smiles, but made sure to hold in their laughter.

She practiced the sign a few times then turned and left the coatroom. Something about the name sign felt very familiar. She sat at her desk and put the thought aside. She then picked up her cell phone and went back to scrolling.

"Give me a name sign!" Sandra insisted.

"You have one," Hassan said.

Shut up, Luis signed.

"What you call me?" Sandra asked threateningly.

Luis knew he was going to have to be the one to show her the name sign. He thought about making something up, like putting his closed fist, the sign for the letter S, to his chin. A very basic name sign.

The most common type of name sign uses the first letter of a person's name placed on either the chin or the forehead. A sign by your chin means you're signing something feminine. Mom, sister, grandmother, daughter are all signed by your chin. Signs on or around your forehead are male signs. Father, brother, grandfather, son and so on.

His reaction to Hassan made it obvious that Sandra's name sign had more meaning. All week long, he thought about telling her how he felt. He wanted to tell her that he liked her. Although this was not how he imagined the conversation, he knew that was exactly what was about to happen.

Using the *S* handshape, Luis circled his fist around his face.

Sandra retreated. Her first assumption was that her name sign had something to do with her arm. Still, she remained suspicious.

"What's that mean?" she asked.

Hassan made a similar motion with his hand, but instead of balling his fist to make an *S*, he started with an open palm and closed his fingers together after encircling his face.

"Pretty," Hassan said, afraid of how Sandra might react.

"Pretty?" she asked Luis in an ironically aggressive manner stepping toward him.

With his eyes wide, Luis nodded nervously.

Poking her finger squarely into Luis's chest Sandra said, "You think that's funny?"

I'm not being-funny! *I'm not-teasing-you!* Luis frantically signed keeping one eye on Hassan, the betrayer.

"You think I'm stupid? Maybe you make fun of them other kids in sign language, but not me! You feel me?" Sandra insisted.

Luis repeated the signs, insisting he wasn't teasing Sandra.

"I don't like it. Change it!" Sandra demanded.

After thinking about it for a moment, Luis reached toward his chest with two open palms and quickly pulled them out in front of his body, balling his fists to punctuate the movement.

"I get it!" said Hassan.

"What's it mean? Nothing dumb this time, either," Sandra warned the boys.

"This is S," Hassan said holding up his fists. Repeating the motion once again he said, "For Sandra."

"I know that one," she said impatiently.

Hassan repeated Luis's motion exactly and said, "This mean strong."

"Strong?" Sandra thought about the word before attempting the sign for herself.

"Strong," she said again. "Okay, bet! That's good."

"I know my name sign," Rian said, turning their attention her way.

She crossed her fingers on her right hand and made the letter *R*. As she brought the hand to her head Luis tensed up. Suddenly he felt ashamed of the name sign he had given her.

To his surprise, instead of placing her crossed fingers behind her ear, Rian twirled them down in a spiral motion from her temple to her shoulder, mimicking the name sign Luis made up for her the day they met at the mall.

"What's that mean? He said you're crazy or something?" Sandra asked.

"No, it's for my hair," Rian said. "Luis gave me that name sign the day we met at the mall. Remember?"

Relieved, Luis nodded in agreement.

Rian could sense Luis's worry about the name sign. For a moment, she thought about calling him out for being so mean to her in the first weeks of school. She chose instead to focus on the fact that they were getting along. Recess spent with Luis, Hassan, Wayne and Sandra was quickly becoming her favorite part of the day.

Luis recognized Rian's gesture and smiled at her as if to thank her. His feelings for her had changed. He didn't hate her or resent her. He no longer cared that she had a cochlear implant. She was cool. They were friends.

15

TIMOTHY ROLLINS

John Hancock, nestled in the center of Millbrook Park, was the kind of neighborhood school that educated generations of locals. The school enjoyed old traditions considered as rites of passage for students. One of those traditions was Mrs. Miller's sixth-grade tile project. The end of October marked the beginning of tile season.

Mrs. Miller, Hancock's art teacher for 36 years, taught her sixth-grade students how to design and fire 4×4 ceramic tiles. Each student's original slab, by year's end, became part of a large mosaic that ornamented the halls of the school. It was a gift from the graduating class, secured to John Hancock Elementary School's walls forever.

Mrs. Miller was a small lady, standing just five feet tall. A large red headband kept the bounce of her curly salt-and-pepper hair in check. Loud patterns on her short-sleeved button-down shirt clashed with her olive green capris that clashed with her rainbow striped knee high socks. Her personality was as loud as her outfits.

Her Art room was uncommon, not because of the years of student artwork pasted to the walls or the containers of paint brushes and sponges. It was because the room took on her haphazard personality. There were oddities that she collected over her career at the school: conversion van accessories, disembodied mannequin parts, fluorescent rolls of tape reserved for road construction jobs, metal machinery parts, old maps of places no longer in existence. There were even large sheets of aluminum piled in a corner. Much of it sat untouched for decades. The centerpiece of the room was the kiln. The kiln was Mrs. Miller's pride and joy.

It was a huge blue behemoth. It stood six feet high and stretched five feet across. An equally large rectangular door inset with stacked insulated white firebrick sealed a cathedral shaped opening, also lined with white ceramic blocks.

A tall, stainless steel chimney sprouted from the top of the blue beast and disappeared into the drop ceiling above. The inside was a cavernous pit of heat, large enough to house a small group of sixth graders.

For decades, the kiln fired tiles for every sixth-grade student that passed through the halls of John Hancock. The only class that did not have a tile display commemorating their time at the school was the class of 1987. No one knew why there was no tile display for that class, it just didn't exist. Every year Mrs. Miller was asked the question, and every year she refused to provide any details.

That day, late in October, Mrs. Miller stood at a long tall table. She wore an apron and held a rolling pin in her right hand. On the table in front of her sat a 10-pound brick of soft pottery clay, wrapped neatly in a thin plastic bag.

"This is clay," she said to the class, opening the plastic cover and pulling out the gray mass. "Specifically, it is raw clay. I am going to show you how to cut squares from it. These squares will eventually become your tiles."

She threw the clay onto a large piece of canvas resting on the hard surface of the table below. She cut a piece of the soft gray brick and added a little water to it.

"When you add water to the clay you get something called slip." She played with the clay slip, letting it slide between her fingers, allowing gray water to run down her wrist.

"After I roll this clay, I want it about a quarter of an inch thick." As she spoke, Mrs. Miller rolled the clay slab with her rolling pin. "Any thinner than that, it won't fire right."

She turned the canvas ninety degrees and continued to roll the clay.

"Does anyone know who the first people were to fire clay into household objects?" She asked, her eyes down, never leaving the table.

"Your parents," Shack whispered to Ben Ellis at the back of the circle surrounding the demonstration.

"Incorrect, Mr. Shack," her comment heaved his way without her ever pulling her eyes off the clay. "It was the Mesopotamians."

"Now, I'm going to cut off a piece with my knife. If you don't roll the clay properly your square will actually turn into a rectangle when you fire it."

Using an exacto knife, and without any measuring instrument, Mrs. Miller cut a perfect 4 × 4 square from the clay.

"There," she said, holding it up for all to see.

"Any questions?" she asked.

"What happened in 1987?" asked Reg Mosley.

Mrs. Miller wiped a bead of sweat from her brow and answered, "A lot of things happened in 1987, Reginald. President Reagan gave his Berlin Wall speech, Jim Baker got caught up in that scandal, the Lost Boys came out. You'll have to be more specific."

"I mean the tiles. Why didn't the class of 1987 make tiles?" Reg replied, a little embarrassed.

"I figured that's what you meant. The class of 1987 didn't do tiles. There's no story, it just didn't happen. Are there any questions about working with clay?"

"Is it tile time already?" Mr. Herman asked from the back of the classroom as he shuffled over to the group. "How exciting. Where are you putting them up this year, Robin?"

"Probably in the stairwell by the recess yard. I'm going to have to retire soon, I'm running out of wall space in this building." Mrs. Miller and Mr. Herman laughed. Neither had interest in retiring anytime soon.

Back in his classroom, the students watched Mr. Herman solve word problems on the tiny chalkboard space flanking the Smart Board.

"Will owns a farm. On this farm he grows squash, turnips, and beets. If one-sixth of his crops are beets and five-twelfths are turnips, what fraction of his crops are squash?"

Despite the fact the word problem was already in front of every student in the room, courtesy of their consumable math journal, Mr. Herman insisted on writing every word of the question on the board. By the time he was finished scrawling the problem in the margins around the Smart Board, most everyone in the class had already solved it.

"Did you know, the first jack-o-lanterns were made from turnips?" In any other class, this question would have caught the students off guard, but in Mr. Herman's room it was only a matter of time before the topic changed from Math to whatever he felt like talking about.

"It's true. The tradition of carving turnips started in Ireland of all places. You see, the legend goes there was a man the villagers called Stinky Jack…."

Uninterested in Stinky Jack and the origins of the jack-o-lantern, Reg Mosley decided to change the topic.

"Mr. Herman, do you know why there are no tiles for the class of 1987?" he asked.

Mr. Herman's face pinched with enthusiasm.

"You don't know about Timothy Rollins?" he asked.

The class looked around at one another. This was a name they did not know.

"Well… I will tell you, but you all must promise not to tell Mrs. Miller that I said anything. It's a sore subject for her."

For the first time in weeks, Mr. Herman's class sat up in anticipation for something he was about to say.

"There once was a sixth-grade boy named Timothy Rollins. He was a normal boy. He rode his bike to school, he had a small group of friends. He was a quiet young man. He had these glasses, though. They were thick, like bottle glass. His vision was very bad. The glasses made his eyes look very large."

Mr. Herman's hands spread out before his face, emphasizing the point.

"The other kids in the school called him Kermit on account of the largeness of his eyes. He hated the nickname, but he was a small kid and didn't rock the boat. So he just accepted it," he told them.

"Couldn't he just wear contacts?" Elisha asked.

"One day in late October, Kermit, or Timothy, up and disappeared. He asked to be excused to go to the bathroom, and he never returned," said Mr. Herman, pacing the room as he spoke.

"At first, they assumed he left the building. Went home. They were prepared to suspend him. Problem is, he didn't go home. The day came and went, but Timothy was nowhere to be found.

"The next day the police were out looking for him. And the next day and the day after that. He just vanished."

Jamilah raised her hand and asked, "What does this have to do with the tiles?"

"I'm getting there, Jamilah," Mr. Herman said coyly. "You need to hear the whole story."

"What happened to him?" asked Rian, fascinated.

"Well, Rain, they were never able to say, conclusively, since they never found his body. At least, they couldn't identify what they assume was his body!"

The class gasped. Rian was so astonished, for once it didn't even bother her that Mr. Herman still called her Rain.

"The rest of the story has never been proven. According to legend, Timothy did go to the bathroom but when he got there, another boy named

Teddy Lombardo was there too. Lombardo was a bully. The worst of the worst. He was the kind of kid that's too scared to go after kids his own size. He was in the bathroom giving another boy, Rupert Dando, a swirly."

"What's a swirly?" asked Lucas.

"Well, that's unimportant. Let's just say it involved a toilet and Mr. Dando's head." The imagery sparked immediate laughter from everyone in the room.

Mr. Rose interjected, "Do you really think this story is appropriate, Mr. Herman?"

"They need to hear this," Mr. Herman said, throwing a subtle wink in Mr. Rose's direction. He continued. "This is local history. Millbrook lore! Once Timothy realized what he walked in on, he turned and ran out of the bathroom. Lombardo, afraid Timothy would go to an adult about what he saw, chased after him, grabbed him by his shirt collar and knocked off his glasses.

"Timothy wiggled out of Lombardo's grasp and ran. He couldn't see where he was going without the glasses, but he soldiered on anyway, trying to find a place to hide. Eventually, he saw a dark classroom and ran inside. It was Mrs. Miller's Art room."

On cue, the class let out another gasp.

"He fumbled around the room and ran into things, making lots of noise. Eventually, he found his way to the kiln. In the dark, Timothy thought it was a closet and pushed his way inside."

Mr. Herman paused, anticipating another gasp from the class, but this time there was none. He continued with the story.

"Lombardo wasn't fooled. He saw Timothy duck in the Art room and hide in the kiln. He even called out, 'I know you're in there, Kermit. You didn't see anything. Right?' Timothy didn't answer. That made Lombardo mad. He closed the door and locked Timothy inside the kiln. Then he left."

"How do you know this?" asked Elisha. "I mean, if the police never solved it…"

"My dear, I started working here at Hancock Elementary school in 1967. I've been here over 50 years. Do you think there is anything I don't know about this school?"

The class looked around at one another, acknowledging the wisdom coming from this man. A truly remarkable elder, who, they agreed knew all there was to know about John Hancock Elementary School.

"That was Friday afternoon. Timothy was stuck in there all weekend. On Monday morning, Mrs. Miller wasted no time firing up that kiln. The clay pieces she left in there had been drying for a while, and she figured it was time to cook 'em!"

Another gasp filled the room.

"Does anyone know the temperature a kiln is set to in order to fire clay? Anyone?" Mr. Herman paused and scanned the room and saw no hands raised.

"One thousand eight hundred degrees," he said. "One thousand eight hundred degrees is the same temperature you use to cremate a body."

Shrieks of horror filled the room.

"All that was left of poor Kermit, was a pile of ash. Well, I suppose I've said enough. Too much perhaps. None of this has ever been proven, you know. You can see why you must never say anything to Mrs. Miller. To this day she remains racked with guilt."

"You're making this up," Shack called out from his seat in the back of the class.

"I wish I was, Gerard. I knew Timothy. He was in my class. I've heard him. Late at night, I've heard his voice echo down the halls," Mr. Herman was wrapping up the tale, when Luis raised his hand to ask a question.

"What did he say?" Mr. Rose spoke, voicing for Luis.

"He wants his glasses. He roams the halls looking for them. He remembers Lombardo took them and he says, 'Give them back. Give them back! Give them back!'"

Each time Mr. Herman said the words, the volume and intensity in his voice increased, rising to a climax.

That afternoon in late October, the legend of Timothy Rollins was passed on to Mr. Herman's sixth-grade class, and it would remain in their minds the rest of the day.

16

THE DANCE

That year, Halloween fell on a Saturday which meant the annual Hancock Halloween Dance was on a Friday night. Everyone in the fifth and sixth grade was there, the only classes invited to the party.

Except for a table set up for students to buy Halloween treats and another one serving as a landing spot for Mr. Tasker to play the role of DJ, most of the long lunch tables in the cafetorium were folded into their upright positions and moved out of the way to make room for the decorations and dance floor.

Clusters of black and orange balloons floated around the room. Black, silhouetted cut-outs of cats, witches, and ghosts were taped to the walls, and a giant Paper Mache pumpkin stood beside DJ Tasker's turntables. The music was pumping, and the students, dressed up in their Halloween costumes, were ready to party.

Well, they were almost ready to party. The dance floor was filled with girls while the boys huddled together in small groups as far from the dance floor as possible. Luis, Hassan, and Wayne stood together at the snack table, shoveling handfuls of candy corn into their mouths.

Luis was dressed as Batman's arch nemesis, the Joker. His face was covered in white face paint. Red lipstick stretched from ear to ear, and his hair was colored green. A vinyl purple suit jacket with an orange flower on the oversized lapel hung carelessly over a white button-down shirt finished with a green bowtie.

The matching purple pants were not surrounded by the walking boot, which was no longer needed according to the doctor. His ankle was healed, and Luis was ready to dance.

Wayne wore a black bodysuit with bright white skeleton bones printed on the chest, pelvis, sleeves, and legs. Instead of a mask the outfit had a hood that zipped all the way up over his face. His hands were covered with white gloves.

Hassan was dressed as a werewolf. His outfit consisted of a red flannel shirt, torn jeans, a furry Wolfman mask and matching paw gloves. The mask made it difficult for him to see his friends, and the gloves made it impossible for him to sign. Eating the candy corn was also a chore, but he managed to get that large furry glove up under the mask and most of the candy into his mouth.

Among the handful of girls not dancing were Sandra and Rian. They stood together against the wall drinking punch and making fun of other people's costumes. Rian was dressed in a black hoodie with a red felt black widow mark stitched across the front. Three sets of spider legs descended from either arm, bound together by ribbon sewn in from the sleeve at the elbow and the wrist. This allowed her to move all eight legs at the same time.

She wore tights with a spider web pattern billowing down each leg, and her hair had cotton-like threads, resembling webs, worked into her red curls.

Sandra's outfit was modest in its execution. A headband with cat ears rested atop her head, and three whiskers were drawn just above her lips in black eye liner. A black sweater and black tights finished the outfit.

"Check out Lucas," Sandra said, pointing at the boy.

Lucas was dressed as a maniac clown. His white shirt had black sleeves, a ruffled black collar, and fat red pom-pom buttons on the front. The pants had large black and white stripes running down the legs. His face was done in greasepaint and a wig was designed to make the red curls on either side of the bald scalp resemble horns. The outfit was, of course, splattered with blood.

106

"He looks like he should be hanging out in the sewer with Pennywise!" Sandra said, laughing along with Rian.

"Whose Henny Wise?" asked Rian.

"No, I said Pennywise," Sandra repeated, overemphasizing the *P* in Penny. "Didn't you see It?"

"See what?" asked Rian.

"It. The movie. With the clown?"

"It's hard to hear anything in here. The music is so loud," Rian admitted. Usually she was uncomfortable admitting when she had a hard time understanding, but with Sandra, it didn't bother her.

They made fun of the other students' costumes, they laughed at the way they danced, and they made jokes at the boys grazing around the food. Basically, they were having a blast.

On the other side of the cafetorium, Luis was stewing over how and when to ask Sandra to dance. He had already missed a pair of slow dance opportunities, and he was concerned there weren't many left.

"Just go ask her for to dance," Hassan's muffled voice and awkward signing was starting to annoy Wayne and Luis.

"What?" Wayne asked impatiently. "I can't understand you!"

Hassan removed the wolf gloves to make signing easier and repeated his suggestion.

O-K, Luis signed, trying to act like he wasn't nervous.

"You want us to ask?" Hassan suggested pointing back and forth between himself and Wayne.

He knew it was a copout, but Luis had never asked a girl to dance before, and he really wanted to dance with Sandra. After a moment, he nodded to Hassan and Wayne who wasted no time heading over to the girls.

When the boys got close enough for Rian and Sandra to recognize them, Sandra burst out laughing.

"What's so funny?" demanded Wayne.

"Look at you. Hassan looks like a dog, and you look like his bone." Sandra's joke made Rian laugh and Sandra laugh even harder. Hassan and Wayne turned to each other and inspected each other's outfits. They were not amused.

"Yeah, you know what you look like?" Wayne asked defensively.

Sandra stopped laughing immediately. Her expression was suddenly and unexpectedly threatening. She stepped up to Wayne and with her fist balled she asked, "What do I look like?"

Backing away, Wayne said, "A cat."

"Where's Luis?" Rian asked, trying to change the topic and play the role she loved, peacemaker.

"He is in back," Hassan said, but no one heard him. His muffled voice barely registered.

Hassan removed the mask and wiped his brow. His black hair was matted to his forehead and he took a deep inhale of the fresh air in the room.

"Hi, Hassan," Rian said excitedly. "I like your costume. It's very scary."

"Thanks," Hassan said while taking another inhale of fresh cafetorium air.

"You are makora?" Hassan asked.

"What's that?" asked Rian.

"I don't know the word, you are..." Hassan trailed off.

"A spider!" Rian exclaimed.

"Spider. Your costume is very good," said Hassan.

"Thanks!" Rian replied excitedly. "My mom made it for me. So where's Luis?"

"He want to know if Sandra will…" Hassan trailed off, finding he was nervous asking Sandra to dance too.

"What's he want?" Sandra asked.

"The next song, he want to dance," said Hassan.

"So? He can dance. He don't need my permission," said Sandra.

"No stupid, he wants to dance with you," said Wayne, who immediately regretted calling Sandra stupid.

She lunged at Wayne who backed away. She kept coming, and he kept retreating.

"Stupid? Who you calling stupid, Milk-Bone?" asked Sandra.

"Wait," said Rian. "Are you going to say yes?"

"Am I going to dance? With Luis?" Sandra's question bought her a minute to consider the request. She didn't know how to dance and had never been asked by a boy.

The request was a pleasant surprise to Sandra who was starting to like Luis. She thought he was cute, and she loved spending recess learning to sign with him. For a split second she considered saying yes.

"No," she answered.

Rian turned to Sandra and said, "You should do it. I think he really likes you."

"He can't dance," proclaimed Sandra.

"Lou can dance," Hassan interjected, but Sandra wasn't buying it.

"He's deaf. How can he dance, when he can't hear music?" she asked.

"I don't know, but he can dance. I watch him do it," Hassan replied as the good soldier fighting for a lost cause.

"Nah, you outta pocket. I'm not dancing with him," Sandra said as she walked away.

Rian suspected that there was more to Sandra's decision than Luis's dancing skills, but she left it alone. If Sandra wanted to talk about boys, she would talk about boys.

"Forget this," said Wayne turning around and heading back to the candy corn table.

"What are you going to tell Luis?" Rian asked Hassan.

Hassan shrugged, "I just tell him what she say."

"You can't tell him that. It will hurt his feelings. It's not his fault he can't dance. How can you dance when you can't hear music?" Rian said.

"I am true. Lou can dance! I will go tell him," Hassan said, turning and following Wayne.

When he returned he told Luis exactly what Sandra said. Defeated, Luis handed his empty paper cup to Miss Hughes, who was working the punch bowl, folded his arms and leaned against the wall.

Miss Hughes had been eavesdropping on the conversation, watching what the boys were signing. Her heart hurt for Luis, so she decided to offer some advice.

Miss Hughes had worked with Luis for three years. As a reward for hard work, she would let him choose games to play on an old Wii system she kept in her classroom on Friday afternoons. One day, instead of playing his normal choice, Super Smash Brothers, he chose Just Dance 2016. She remembers being shocked at how well he followed the dancer on the screen, hitting every move on the beat in song after song.

Miss Hughes walked from behind the table and signed to Luis, voice off. This was something she sometimes did to make conversations a little more private.

You-should-dance-to the song-from-that game! Miss Hughes signed excitedly. *Show her-your skills*!

110

Luis dismissed her. He grabbed another cup and hid his face behind it, slowly sipping his punch.

"Yeah Lou. You want all them to think Deaf means you can't dance? You show everyone you can do it!" Hassan chimed in.

Luis finished his punch and placed the empty cup on the table. He smiled at Miss Hughes and walked to the front of the cafetorium.

Luis approached the DJ table where he found Mr. Tasker wearing sunglasses, a Hawaiian shirt, a straw hat, and a straw skirt. As the song he was playing ended, he turned his attention to Luis.

"What can I do you for, Luis?" Mr. Tasker asked, grabbing a pen and a napkin for him to write on.

Luis scribbled furiously and handed his request back to Mr. Tasker. Needing the light from his cell phone to understand the message, he saw that Luis had written the words "I Gotta Feeling" on the napkin.

Mr. Tasker dug through his ancient collection of CDs and grabbed a disk by the Black Eyed Peas. Flanking the front of the cafetorium were dual Fender speakers, approximately three feet high. Luis positioned himself a few feet from one, and when the song started, he stood still and felt the music. He could not hear the melody, but the bass from the speaker pumped out a familiar rhythm that, when close enough to the speakers, Luis felt pulse through his body.

Nerves caused him to forget the start of the Just Dance routine he'd done a thousand times before, but halfway through the first verse he got his footing and started to move.

At first, his movements were small and self-conscious. He felt shy allowing other people to watch him, but as the song continued his comfort level grew, and by the first chorus he was killin' it.

It didn't take long for a group of girls standing near Luis to take notice. He was the only boy on the dance floor, and if polled, he would have been picked last by his peers to be the boy they expected to get out there and move. But not only was Luis able to dance, he was good.

A minute into the song, students began to encircle Luis and cheer him on. Rian, who suddenly felt embarrassed about her claim that he could not dance was astounded by what she saw.

She grabbed Sandra and pulled her in the direction of the dance floor. "You have to see this!" she said excitedly. "Luis is dancing. He's really good."

Sandra followed Rian to a large group of students encircling Luis. Pushing their way into the perimeter, they stood stunned, watching Luis command the room.

As the crowd grew, and onlookers expanded the circle's radius, Luis kept his eyes out for Sandra. When he saw her watching, he smiled at her, catching her off guard. She found herself smiling right back at him.

The music had taken over. He was smooth. When he hit a pose, it was clean and exact. The beat coursed through his arms, legs, and body. He didn't need to hear the music, he was the music. He was the bass, the drum, the beat. Even his heart seemed to follow the rhythm of the song. He owned the moment, and Sandra took notice.

When it was over, everyone cheered. They slapped Luis's back. They bumped his fist and gave him the international sign for a good job, holding their thumbs up. He felt like a superstar.

With a newfound confidence, Luis walked over to Sandra and Rian.

"That was awesome!" Rian exclaimed. "How did you do that? I mean, how can you dance when you can't hear the music?" she asked with Hassan's help.

Luis swiped his bent middle finger up his chest, and Hassan said, "Lou can feel the music."

"Not bad," Sandra exclaimed, the closest she could come to complimenting him.

Dance? Luis signed to her.

"You want to dance with Lou?" Once again Hassan voiced for Luis, but he didn't have to. Sandra understood Luis's question loud and clear.

"I don't dance," she insisted.

Luis threw out a sign with his right fist, pointing at everyone, Sandra, Rian, Hassan, and Wayne.

"He say all us dance," Hassan said to the group.

"Okay!" Rian answered excitedly. After watching Luis, she wanted to join the other kids on the dance floor. Hassan and Wayne joined reluctantly, but Sandra didn't move.

"Come on," said Rian as she started dancing to the music.

She, Luis, Wayne, and Hassan danced, but it was nothing like the show Luis had put on. Their movements were small, awkward and off rhythm, not unlike the majority of the other students dancing all around them.

The song finished, and another played, as the group of four danced and Sandra looked on.

"Ya'll corny," she called out.

Breaking from the group, Luis walked over to Sandra and held out his hand. She looked suspiciously at it and shook her head no. Refusing to give up, Luis moved his hand to his chest.

Please, he voiced the word as he signed.

Defeated, Sandra extended her hand. Luis grasped it and pulled her to the group. At first, she stood with her friends but refused to move. Then, her favorite song, "Havana," filled the room. The final push she needed. Sandra started to move her body to the music. As she danced she looked at Luis, and he looked back at her. They were both dancing. They were dancing together.

17

HALLOWEEN

For the first time in his life Luis was allowed to trick or treat in Millbrook Park with his friends. Rhawnhurst was not far from Mayfair, Hassan's neighborhood. Hassan's father offered to drive Luis home so they could be together. After the disappointing end to Luis's basketball season it was easy to get Jennifer to agree to the plan.

Wayne caught the Market Frankford train from his house to Millbrook Park to meet up with the boys. Luis and Hassan were envious of the freedom Wayne enjoyed. No one at his house cared whether he came or went. No one asked where he was going or what time he'd be home. At twelve, he was the most independent person they knew.

They got an early start, knocking on their first door by five o'clock. They winded their way through cul-de-sac after cul-de-sac with surgical precision. All the homes in Millbrook Park were duplexes and row homes which maximized their ability to collect as much candy as quickly as possible. After one hour their bags were full.

They worked their way up Millbrook Avenue, eventually arriving at Aunt Nancy's house. When they rang the doorbell, Rian answered holding a bowl full of Kit-Kats. She was dressed in her spider outfit.

"Ticker Treat," Hassan spoke, stopping abruptly when he saw Rian come to the door. "Rian, this is your house?"

"It's my aunt's house. I live here," she said, a little embarrassed.

"You're not trick or treating?" asked Wayne.

"I wanted to, but I don't have anyone to go with. Mom doesn't want me to go alone, and I'm too old to go with her, so I'm handing out candy instead. Kit-Kat?" Rian held the bowl out for her friends.

Luis, Wayne, and Hassan plunged their hands into the bowl clawing handfuls of the chocolate wafer candy. They tossed it into their bags. Hassan dropped his Kit-Kats into one of the large furry Wolfman paws. He was using it as a second candy bag since the one he started with was filled to the top.

"Later," said Wayne, heading down the steep front steps. Hassan followed close behind. They did not waste time chatting with anyone, even friends.

"Bye," Rian waved to Luis watching her friends descend the front steps of Aunt Nancy's house.

Wait, Luis signed to Hassan and Wayne, who reluctantly climbed back up the steps.

Luis signed something to Wayne. Rian recognized a couple of the signs he used. She saw him sign the word *want* and the word *us*, but the word in between she didn't know.

"Join us? For tricker treats," asked Hassan.

"Yes," Rian belted out her answer before Hassan could finish asking the question. She skipped down a few steps to meet them and then stopped in her tracks.

"I have to ask my mom," she said, bounding back up the steps and into the house.

"Hurry," Wayne yelled to an empty doorway.

Rian ran into the kitchen where Joanna and Nancy sat finishing their dinner.

"Mom, some friends of mine are at the door. They want me to go trick or treating with them. Can I go?" Rian asked.

"I don't know. I'm not crazy about you walking around the neighborhood without an adult," replied Joanna.

"Come on. I'm twelve years old. All the other kids in my class are out with their friends," she said.

"You don't know that," said Joanna.

"Yes, I do. They've all come to the house tonight. I've given candy to Stuart Houser, Elisha, Jamilah, and Evander. I don't want to be stuck here all night. Please?"

Her voice was desperate and impatient. She knew the boys weren't going to wait long for her.

"Come on, Jo," said Aunt Nancy. "We walked with our friends at her age."

"It was different for us," said Joanna.

"How?" asked Nancy.

"The world was safer when we were kids," Joanna said confidently.

"Bull," said Nancy. "Try again."

"Well, we weren't walking around Philadelphia. We were in the suburbs."

"Jo, this is her home now. I don't know how long you two are going to be here with me, but the kids knocking on my door are her classmates. Millbrook Avenue is her street. This is her neighborhood. Look at her."

Nancy turned and looked at Rian affectionately as she spoke.

"She's a good kid. She has friends. This is a perfectly safe neighborhood. Stop being such a snob."

"A snob?" Joanna repeated indignantly. "I'm not being a snob!"

"Sure you are. Most of you suburbanites are. Here's the thing though, you're not a suburbanite anymore," replied Nancy.

"Yeah, Mom," said Rian. "We're city folk!"

116

"City folk? So I'm just supposed to let her go roam around the neighborhood?" Joanna asked.

"Not without meeting her friends first. Come on, Ri," Nancy rose from her seat and turned to her sister. "Introduce us to your friends."

Rian was relieved to see Luis, Hassan, and Wayne still standing on the porch when she came out of the kitchen. She ran to the door and opened it.

"My mom wants to meet you guys. I promise it will only take a minute," Rian spoke directly to Hassan, her eyes begging him to translate for Luis, and do so quickly. She felt the urgency to go as much as her friends.

She held open the screen door, and the three walked into the house.

"Your friends are boys?" Joanna asked the obvious question.

"Yes, Mom. This is Luis, Hassan, and Wayne." Luis was looking at Hassan who translated for Rian.

"Your friends are deaf?" Joanna asked abruptly.

Embarrassed by Joanna's bluntness, Rian turned to her mother and gave her a look that begged her to not chase them away.

"Hi, I am Rian's Aunt Nancy." Aunt Nancy said, holding her hand out to shake Hassan's. She pulled it back awkwardly, realizing he was fingerspelling her name for Luis. She stepped back to let him finish.

"I am Hassan," he said and turned to Luis. "This is Lou."

"Hello, Lou," said Nancy. "It's nice to meet you."

Hassan turned to translate, but Luis shot his index up and signed, *I-understand*.

Nice-to meet-you, Luis signed to Nancy.

"I'm Wayne," said Wayne. "We ready?"

"I'm not sure about this, Ri. It's getting dark, and I'm not sure it's safe to send you out without an adult." Joanna spoke apologetically.

"We just talked about this?" Rian said exasperated.

"Yeah Jo, we did," said Nancy.

"Mind your own business, Nancy," Joanna shot back at her sister.

Rian turned to Luis and held up her index finger, begging him to give her one more minute. Luis nodded, and Wayne folded his arms in frustration. Rian pulled her mother back into the kitchen.

"Mom, please let me go. I don't want to hand out candy. It's Halloween. I want to trick or treat."

"You didn't tell me that your friends were deaf," said Joanna.

"So? Why is that a problem?" asked Rian.

"It's just… I thought your friends were… not deaf," said Joanna.

"Who cares if they are deaf? I mean, I'm deaf. Why shouldn't my friends be deaf?" Rian was as surprised as her mother that she had just defined herself as deaf.

"You're not deaf!" Joanna insisted. "You're hearing impaired."

"Oh really?" Rian asked incredulously.

She reached behind her ear and pulled off her implant.

"What am I now?"

Joanna, visibly upset, was pointing and gesturing and making her case for why Rian was not deaf. Rian heard none of it. She stood there with her implant in her hand, unable to understand a word of what her mother was saying.

"Put that back on!" Joanna demanded.

Rian placed the implant back behind her ear.

"I knew this was a mistake. I never should have brought you here. You're confused," said Joanna.

"No, I'm not. I'm lonely. These are my friends. I've tried to make other friends, but they are the ones who talk to me. Or, at least, sign to me. They're really nice, and I want to go with them. Please, Mom."

Nancy was standing in the doorway.

"They're about to leave," said Nancy, looking at Joanna with the judgmental stare only a sister can offer a sister.

"What if I came with you?" asked Joanna.

"Mom!" Rian's one word objection put that idea to rest immediately.

"Jo, they seem like nice boys. They're kids. Let Rian be a kid," said Nancy.

Joanna looked at the clock, which read 6:20.

"I want you back by eight o'clock," said Joanna.

"Really?" Rian asked, her expression changing from despair to delight. "Okay, I promise. I'll be back by eight."

"And Rian, we're going to continue this conversation another time. You're not deaf," she said to her daughter.

Signing for herself, Rian imitated something she saw Luis sign the first day they met in Miss Hughes room. Placing her index finger to her ear and her mouth she said, "I'm deaf not Deaf," fingerspelling the second word with a capital *D*.

Hassan poked his head in the kitchen, and with his fingers crossed on both hands he signed, *Ready?*

Rian looked at Joanna, who looked at Nancy. Nancy nodded at Joanna as if to say, "It's okay. Let her go."

"Eight o'clock," said Joanna.

They turned and ran out of the kitchen and through the front door. Rian was at the bottom of the steps when she heard Joanna's voice call out to her, "You need a bag!"

119

Rian turned and looked up at the top of the steps. Joanna took the hollow plastic pumpkin holding the candy and dumped it onto a table. She held it out to Rian.

"Here."

"Hurry!" insisted Wayne.

Rian ran up the steps and grabbed it from her mother.

"Thanks, Mom."

"Be safe," Joanna said, as she watched her daughter dart down the steps, join her friends and disappear into the Halloween night.

They knocked on 38 doors in one hour. They knocked on the last door four times, completely ignoring the fact the porch light was off. Accepting they had reached their end, the four sat on a curb at the top of Millbrook Ave., opened their bags, and rejoiced in their bounty.

"Who got Nerds? I need Nerds," Wayne asked.

"I got a box," Hassan pulled a small box of grape-flavored Nerds out of his bag.

"Give you Twix for it?" Wayne said.

"Deal," Hassan snatched the Twix bar out of Wayne's hand.

Luis fingerspelled W-A-W-A and pointed to the convenience store across the street.

"Wawa!" Hassan said excitedly.

At the corner of Millbrook and Academy was a small strip mall that housed a laundromat, Cicero's Bakery, Crown Deli, and an insurance office. Just past the strip mall, right on the corner, was a small stand-alone building with the name "Wawa" written in large red illuminated letters over the door. Next to its name, was another light, shaped in the likeness of a Canada goose flying across a tri-colored plastic sun.

A little food mart with great coffee, sandwiches, donuts, and whatever else you might need in a jiffy, Wawa was a fan favorite in the neighborhood. Wayne and Hassan needed no convincing, but Rian was unsure.

"It's getting late," she said.

"It's not even eight o'clock," said Wayne. "Are you a baby?"

"I'm not a baby. My mom asked me not to stay out late, that's all. I need to get home soon."

Luis watched Hassan as he interpreted Rian's concern.

Five minutes, he signed to her flicking his open palm like the ticking second hand of a clock.

"Five minutes." Hassan translated. "No worry."

18

WAWA

Rian took inventory of the donuts and muffins under the orange tinted warming lights in the display case. Banana nut and chocolate chip muffins were stacked over eclairs which were stacked over jelly donuts.

At the other end of the store, Luis and Hassan were filling twenty-ounce plastic cups with frozen fruit-flavored drinks. Luis pulled the lever for a drink called Raspberry Blues, and Hassan filled his cup with something called Red Riot.

They operated the machine at the same time, occupying the same small space in front of the dispenser. Luis pulled the Raspberry Blues lever from right to left and elbowed Hassan deliberately. Hassan returned fire even though his lever was designed to be pulled away from Luis.

Wayne was busy slathering a soft pretzel with spicy brown mustard by the sandwich station. Across from him stood a man and woman having an animated conversation. Luis noticed them right away. The man's flailing arms were a dead giveaway that they were arguing.

When his cup was full, Luis nudged Hassan to get his attention. Hassan thought it was another attempt to shove him, and so he hit Luis back.

Look! Luis signed.

Hassan turned and saw a scruffy-looking man in an oversized black hoodie and paint-stained jeans point at a woman dressed in flannel pants and a long sleeve 76ers T-shirt. The old, worn-out shirt was emblazoned with the words 2001 NBA Eastern Conference Champions.

Hassan topped off his Red Riot and placed the large cup on the stainless steel ledge below the dispenser. Luis signed the letters *F* and *M* to Hassan, who thought for a moment and reached into the front pocket of his torn jeans and pulled out his FM system.

He turned it on and brought it to his ear. With a press of a button he synced the silver pen-shaped microphone to his hearing aids.

Slowly he moved toward the couple. Careful not to get too close, he slid into the candy aisle and pointed the FM at the two of them. When he was about twenty feet away the FM started to pick up their conversation.

"They'll know we didn't pay. All the paid slips are stamped," the nervous woman wrung her hands as she spoke to the man.

"They won't check. They never do. You think they pay them enough to care?" the man replied, holding a small slip of paper out to the woman.

"Let's just go," the woman pleaded, refusing to take the slip.

"I'm hungry. I want my sandwich. You ain't hungry?" the man asked.

"No," the woman said with certainty.

"Just take it," he demanded, thrusting the slip of paper into the woman's hand.

Hassan interpreted the conversation for Luis. His eyes bulged when he realized these two people were about to commit a crime. They were going to take food without paying for it.

At Wawa, you first order your sandwich at a kiosk in front of the sandwich station. Then you bring your slip to the register on the other side of the store. A cashier must stamp your slip, and when your food is ready, you stick your paid slip into a basket, and take your sandwich. Easy peasy.

Luis figured these two were planning to take the sandwich with an unpaid slip.

"Twenty-one," a man with a hairnet around a thick black beard called out from behind the sandwich counter.

The scruffy-looking man gave the woman a subtle shove, and she stepped forward. Her actions were very conspicuous as she flashed a nervous smile and stuffed the slip deep into the basket, attempting to hide the missing *PAID* stamp.

"Have a good one," the bearded sandwich maker spoke without looking up as he slapped a pile of thinly sliced ham onto a hoagie roll. The woman scooped up the sandwiches, and the pair made a beeline for the door.

Luis and Hassan looked at each other with mouths open. Luis pointed his index finger from his mouth to the clerk behind the register asking Hassan if he thought they should, *Let them know?*

Hassan shrugged. Before they could decide what to do, Rian darted into their aisle, panicked.

"We have to go," she said, pointing toward the door.

"What is wrong?" asked Hassan.

"Shack!" the word fell out of Rian's mouth and landed with a thud.

Hassan signed his name and Luis repeated it, knocking his forehead with a closed fist, signing Shack's name sign. Luis looked left and right scanning the store for him. Rian pointed to the hot dog warmer.

Shack clutched a hot dog in a wet, wrinkled bun. He was smothering it in globs of pasty red ketchup. He was close to Wayne but didn't recognize him in the skeleton costume. Wayne was busy stuffing the remains of his pretzel into his mouth and failed to notice Shack altogether.

"We need to go," she repeated, pointing furiously at the door.

Dealing with Shack at school was bad enough. She didn't want to have any part of him on Halloween.

Luis wasn't concerned. *Follow*, he signed, holding out his thumbs, placing his right fist behind the left and moving them together as if the one were chasing the other.

Hassan turned to Rian and said, "Lou say we follow him."

"Follow who? Shack? Forget it. No way!" Rian whisper-shouted.

"Scared?" Hassan asked, condescendingly.

"It's just a stupid idea," Rian said. "If you want to follow him, go ahead. I'm going home."

Home, she signed, looking directly at Luis.

Luis waved goodbye to her.

Insulted, Rian turned to walk out but stopped when she realized she had to wait for Shack to leave. She wasn't going to risk being seen.

Luis waved his hands dismissively, inviting Rian to keep going, but she stayed in place, never taking her eyes off Shack. She peered over bags of chips and watched as he paid the cashier.

Moments later, he walked out of the store. Luis ran to get Wayne. After explaining the plan to his eager wingman, Wayne hustled to the register to pay for his now fully-eaten pretzel. Luis and Hassan abandoned their frozen drinks completely.

They were heading to the door when suddenly Shack stopped in the middle of the parking lot. The three of them stood exposed in front of a wall of glass covered in oversized advertisements for coffee and cigarettes. With his back to the store, Shack arched his neck skyward and poured a bag of sour gummy bears down his throat. Then he lowered his head and headed back up Millbrook Avenue.

Luis crossed his fingers and signed, *Ready?*

He opened the door and walked out. Hassan and Wayne followed quickly behind. Rian stood glued to the floor, watching her friends walk away until they disappeared behind a Thursday Dollar Dog advertisement pasted to the window glass. Uncertain of what she was doing, Rian bolted out of the store after them.

19

OUIJA

It was easy to remain hidden as they followed Shack up Millbrook Avenue. They were in costume, and the dark night sky provided cover. Shack didn't move quickly so they had to slow their pace in order to keep a safe distance from him. They stayed on the opposite side of the street and hung close to the parked cars along Millbrook Avenue.

Shack met Ben Ellis at the corner of Holmesburg Circle and Millbrook Avenue. Neither was dressed for Halloween, which surprised Luis. Shack didn't look like someone who turned away the opportunity for free candy. Shack and Ben turned left and headed up Holmesburg Circle. Hassan stopped suddenly.

What? signed Wayne.

"Maybe this idea is bad. My dad is waiting," he said.

Rian agreed, "Hassan's right, we should get back. It's getting late. I told my mom I'd be back by eight, and I'm already ten minutes late."

"Then you're already in trouble," said Wayne.

We-need to-keep going, Luis signed.

Holmesburg ran up a steep hill. They watched Shack and Ben as their silhouettes crested the top and then sank slowly back down the other side. Luis continued his pursuit up Holmesburg after them.

"Our parents are going to get mad," said Rian.

"Not mine," Wayne replied.

126

He considered the choice a moment longer, and then ran after Luis. Hassan followed as well. Rian looked up Millbrook Avenue. She could see Aunt Nancy's house from where she stood.

She thought about going back. She'd enter the house, grab Mom's laptop, and watch videos from the comfort of her couch for the rest of the night. Eventually the boys would fill her in on what happened.

She looked at the house, then back up Holmesburg Circle. Luis, Wayne, and Hassan had already disappeared behind the hill. She took a deep breath and ran after her friends.

Holmesburg Circle was a small cul-de-sac. She found Luis and the others standing in front of a tall chain-link fence. They were having an animated discussion.

"Did you lose him?" asked Rian. The hopeful tone in her voice was lost on them.

"This is where he went," said Wayne.

Rian stared at the fence. It was six feet high, taller than all of them. A sign was posted that read, *Private Property, Keep Out!* Behind the fence was a grove of trees.

Wayne reached down to the bottom of the fence post and lifted the corner of the wire barrier. It was no longer attached to the metal pole, leaving an opening large enough for someone to crawl through.

"You're not thinking of going in there? Look, the sign says, keep out!" said Rian.

"That's what we think," said Wayne, looking at Hassan.

Hassan shuffled his feet.

"Maybe we better go. It's late," said Hassan.

Wayne rolled his eyes. "You scared?"

Hassan did not want to admit that he was scared of going into the woods or what his father would do to him for being late. He was acutely aware that Shack was hiding somewhere in that grove of trees.

Luis's fingertips touched the palm of the opposite hand. He bent the fingers at the knuckle three times like table legs about to give way.

Weak, he signed in Hassan's direction.

Luis tucked his bag of candy behind a nearby bush, crouched low, and crawled through the gap Wayne made in the fence.

Wayne turned to Hassan and motioned for him to crawl through the opening. He did so after hiding his candy with Luis's bag. Wayne shoved his candy bag through the fence and turned to Rian. He held out the green wire for her to hold. She rolled her eyes but grabbed hold nonetheless.

Wayne turned his body, squatted down to his knees, and eased himself through to the other side.

Luis and Wayne motioned for Rian to join them.

Your turn, Luis signed to Rian.

Wayne pushed against the fence with his foot to make space for her to crawl through. Rian stashed her plastic pumpkin, now brimming with candy, along with the others. She got down and began to inch her way through the fence.

She was almost through when one of the spider legs on her costume got snagged on the wire. Her first instinct was to pull, but she immediately felt the leg tear from the rest of her costume.

"I'm stuck," she whispered to Wayne.

"Hurry," he replied.

"I'm stuck," she repeated her words a little louder.

"Give your hand," Hassan said, reaching out to her.

She did as he asked, and with a pull he freed her from the fence and the spider leg from her outfit. Rian looked down to see a few sporadic threads hanging from the spot where the leg once dangled.

"You still have seven legs," said Wayne, laughing at the change to her costume.

"Now what?" she asked annoyed.

"Look," Wayne pointed to what looked like a path. There was a spot at the edge of the tree line where the underbrush had been pulverized by size 12 shoes. He walked toward the spot and followed it into the woods. The others followed.

About a hundred feet into the thicket two windows with muted flickering yellow lights shone ahead of them. It was the soft glow of candlelight.

"A house," Hassan whispered. He pulled on Luis's shoulder and turned him around, signing the words without repeating them.

Luis brushed the tip of his middle finger down the back of his fist and signed, *Empty.*

"How do we know?" Hassan's voice changed volume and octave.

Rian put her finger to her mouth to shush him.

They followed the path closer to the house until they were thirty feet away. The candles illuminated the outside yard through the broken windows. They were at the back of the house.

Luis pointed at Hassan and then to the house. Hassan pointed back at Luis. They both turned to Rian.

"What?" she asked.

Luis, once again flipped his thumb toward Rian.

"Your turn," Hassan whispered.

Rian grimaced as she turned and stared at what looked to be a back door.

"Are you crazy? I'm not going in there!" she said.

Luis signed and Hassan translated, "Go to window. Listen."

"I didn't even want to do this," she reminded them.

Luis made a sign on his throat, signing, *Curious?*

129

She was curious. It seemed clear that Shack and Ben were in there. She wanted to know what they were up to, and she knew she was the only one of them who could for sure hear what was going on in there. Reluctantly she moved closer to the house.

How did this happen? Rian wondered. *I was moments away from going home. This was Luis's idea, yet here I am creeping up to this house in the dark. Alone.*

Snap. The breaking of a tree branch under her feet caused her to freeze. She looked at the windows before her and saw the silhouette of someone's head and shoulders appear in the frame. She couldn't move.

The dark night and overgrowth masked her position well. She could see the featureless head in the window pivot right, then left, looking for the culprit. The sound of laughter came from inside the house, and the shadow in the window frame disappeared.

Laughter? Rian thought to herself, distinctly hearing multiple laughs.

Rian crept closer to the blighted old house, placing each footstep gingerly onto the ground below until she was standing an arm's length from the back doorway.

A large piece of plywood had been carelessly removed and shifted to one side of an exposed door frame. It was an opening large enough for someone to enter.

Shards of jagged glass lined the window frames like bared teeth. The window to her right sprouted a spindly sapling, desperately trying to flee the confines of the house. The window to her left glowed brightly in the night. Through the window, she could see shadows cast up to the ceiling that shifted abruptly as someone walked around the room.

She snuck to the other side of the shadowy window and pressed her head and body against the stone facade of the house. A broken piece of stone poked at her back.

She could smell the stale odor of cigarette smoke. For a moment she was afraid there might be adults inside. Reluctantly she turned her head slowly to peer into the room.

She saw three figures sitting on the floor in a mangled shell of a kitchen. A Ouija board sat on the floor in front of them. Ouija is played with a game board decorated with all the letters of the alphabet written large and spaced out across the center and numbers 0 to 9 printed in a straight row below that. In the top left corner of the board is the word *YES* and in the top right corner is the word *NO*. Its stated purpose is to communicate with the dead.

Shack and Ben were in the room. Shack had a cigarette hanging from his lips. There was a girl in there with them. Rian didn't recognize her. She looked older, possibly a seventh grader.

She wore faded jeans frayed from the pockets to the cuff and a plain sleeveless white t-shirt that seemed out of place on the chilly autumn night. Her makeup was caked in thick coats over her eyes, cheeks, and lips, but the makeup did not entirely conceal the pimples dotting her light brown skin. Two tight braids descended from a part down the middle of her head to her shoulders. She was at least as tall as Shack. Both she and Shack were smoking cigarettes.

Rian's good ear was pointed toward the window allowing her to hear what was said, including the girl's name. Janessa.

"Got my chips?" barked Janessa.

Shack dug through a plastic Wawa bag and retrieved Salt and Vinegar potato chips. He tossed them to her, and they landed at her feet. She made no effort to catch them.

"Here," he said.

She picked up the chips and threw them back at him.

"I said barbeque. Those are nasty," Janessa said with a sneer.

Shack shrugged and pulled open the bag. He dug his hand inside and grabbed a handful of chips, burying them all at once in his mouth.

"Your loss," he said, although the muffled message was lost on Rian, his words held prisoner by a mouthful of chips.

He sucked salty chip dust from each of the five fingers on his hand.

"Are we going to do this?" asked Janessa.

"I don't think this is a good idea. My dad told me that Ouija boards attract demons," said Ben. He was holding the planchette, moving it nervously from one hand to the other.

"You believe that?" Shack asked sarcastically. "You think Parker Brothers can summon the devil?"

"No, I just don't think it is a good idea to mess with things we don't understand," Ben replied.

"Well, then Shack should drop out of school," Janessa laughed like an injured bullfrog at her own joke.

"Let's go. Janessa, you and I will go first," Shack spun the board around and scooted next to her.

"How's it work?" she asked.

"Easy. Put your hand on this thing," Shack snatched the planchette out of Ben's hand.

The planchette was shaped like an upside-down heart, with a little clear plastic hole at the top. He put his fingers on the right side of the planchette, and Janessa put her fingers on the left.

"Now what?" she asked.

"I dunno," replied Shack. "We ask it questions?"

"You're pushing too hard," said Ben. "You're only supposed to lightly touch it, so the spirit can guide it."

"You want to do it?" Shack asked, annoyed.

"Do you want it to work?" Ben snapped back, retrieving a little bit of his dignity.

Shack and Janessa hovered their fingers over the planchette.

"Well, ask something," Janessa ordered.

"Uh, OK. You dead?" he asked.

The planchette did not move.

"That was a stupid question. Don't be stupid," said Janessa.

"Fine," Shack took his hands off the planchette to grab another fistful of potato chips.

After filling his mouth and washing the chips back with a bright blue drink, he wiped his hands off on his shirt and returned his fingers to the planchette.

"This is a message to anyone who can hear us from the spirit world," Shack's voice was more somber as he elongated the words in his statement for dramatic effect.

"The spirit world?" Janessa laughed.

"I thought you wanted me to be serious?" he asked.

"I said serious, not corny," she replied.

"This is a message to anyone who is dead and close to us. Are there any spirits in this jawn…I mean room?" Shack's third attempt to summon the dead escaped Janessa's ridicule at last.

There was a brief pause. Shack and Janessa looked at each other, and no one spoke. Then, the planchette slowly moved to the upper left corner of the Ouija board. The clear plastic circle hovered over the word *YES*.

Janessa pulled her hands off the planchette and yelled, "Oh, my god! You did that! I swear to god, you moved that jawn!"

"I swear to god I didn't," said Shack. "I think you moved it."

They laughed nervously.

"Let's keep going." Shack pulled the planchette back to the center of the board and asked, "Are you in the room with us?"

After another pause the planchette started once again to drift to the right corner of the board over the word *YES*.

"This is creeping me out," said Ben.

"Come on. We got one. Let's keep going," Shack said, returning the planchette to the center of the board.

"Is this your house?" he asked, and again the planchette slid up to the word *YES*, this time even faster than before. Janessa shot Shack a glance, and he returned the look.

"Did you die here?" she asked excitedly.

This time the planchette didn't move.

"Hello. Dummy? I asked you a question," she laughed nervously as she spoke.

"Don't call him dummy," insisted Ben. "You will get him angry."

"Whatever," said Janessa with just a bit of attitude.

"Let me ask the questions. It doesn't want to talk to you," said Shack.

"Because you're moving it," Janessa fired back.

"Were you murdered?" he punctuated each word, turning his head around the room, trying to figure out where the ghost might be standing. The words hung in the air as they waited for a response.

The planchette once again moved to the word *YES*.

Janessa ripped her hand off the planchette and pulled it close to her chest.

"Yo, you're messing with me, Shack."

"I'm telling you I'm not doing it. Do you want to stop?" he asked, expressing mild concern.

"I'm not scared, if that's what you mean," Janessa returned her fingers to the planchette. "Next question."

"He says yes to everything," said Ben. "Ask a different question, like what's his name?"

"How you know it's a him?" asked Janessa. "It could be a dead girl."

Shack pulled the planchette back to the center and asked the question, "Who are you?"

There was no movement so he asked a second time. After another pause the planchette moved to the letter *T*. Then to the *I* and then *M*, eventually spelling out the name *T-I-M-O-T-H-Y R-O-L-L-I-N-S*.

Shack and Janessa jumped up, pulling their hands off the planchette. They looked at each other in horror.

"Tell me you're messing with that thing!" demanded Shack.

"I didn't move that jawn. I swear to god. It was you!" Janessa said pointing her finger at him.

"I'm done," said Ben. "I want to get out of here."

"No way. We have to keep going," Shack insisted.

"Who is Timothy Rollins?" asked Janessa.

"He's a kid who got killed at school, back in 1987," said Ben. "This is dangerous. We shouldn't be talking to him."

"Don't be such a baby. That story wasn't real," said Shack.

"Then how do you explain the conversation you're having with him now?" demanded Ben.

"I know. Quick, put your hands back on this thing," Shack said to Janessa. "Timothy Rollins. What is it that you want?"

There was no movement. Ben looked at Shack, Shack looked at Janessa. Janessa looked at the board.

Shack repeated the question, "What do you want?"

The planchette moved quickly around the board, darting from one letter to the next until it spelled the words *my glasses*.

"What are mygl asses?" Shack asked, confused.

"He said 'my glasses,'" Janessa rolled her eyes as she spoke.

"Oh, my god. Just like Mr. Herman said," gasped Ben. "We need to stop this now."

Suddenly, a loud crash pulled their attention from the board to the outside of the house. Wayne was walking toward the window and tripped over a pile of bricks in his path. Rian pulled her face back and pressed herself against the wall.

"Something's out there!" cried Ben.

"It's probably just an animal," Shack said unconvincingly.

"Yeah, well, go check," said Janessa.

"OK, let's go, Ben," said Shack.

"You go. You're the one he wants to talk to," said Ben.

"It's not a ghost. It's just an animal," Shack insisted.

Wayne lay on the ground looking at Rian. Rian looked at him and wildly waved her hands, cuing him to get up and hide. He crawled behind an overgrown hedge, burying himself in its brambles, making even more noise.

"I heard it again," said Janessa. "Chase it away. I don't want to see no ghost!"

"It's not a ghost. Watch." Shack walked slowly toward the back door.

Rian realized she was in a compromised spot, so she slid around the corner and hid on the side of the house. There was another window into the kitchen on that side. This new perspective allowed her to watch as Shack slowly stepped outside the house. Ben and Janessa crept to the doorway and followed Shack outside.

"Hello? Is somewhere there? If you're hiding, I'm going to find you. And beat you senseless," Shack's threat and the visual of him punching a ghost caused Ben and Janessa to laugh nervously.

Slowly he walked toward the path. He knew it well enough to not need a light.

The bush! Rian thought to herself as she watched Shack near Wayne's hiding spot. *He'll see Wayne. I have to distract him.*

She looked down and saw that a section of the stone wall and mortar that had broken away long ago. It rested in a pile just under the window on the unexposed side of the house. Without much thought, she picked up a large chunk of broken mortar and heaved it into the house through the broken window.

It soared through the kitchen and crashed into a coffee mug sitting on the counter on the opposite wall.

"What was that?" Ben asked in a panic.

"Don't know," Shack answered bewildered. He peered at the kitchen door, still open.

"It came from inside the house! It's in the house!" Janessa yelled.

"I'm not going back in there," said Ben. "Let's get out of here. My parents are going to wonder what happened."

"My bag's in there. You gotta get it! Gerry, get my bag," Janessa ordered.

"Sure," he said nervously. Shack slowly crept back toward the doorway. He could see her large red and black handbag lying on an old table in the center of the room. The Wawa bag sat abandoned on the floor along with the half-finished bag of potato chips.

Acting quickly, Shack ran into the house, grabbed Janessa's handbag, and scooped up the chips. He reached for the plastic Wawa bag but accidentally kicked over the candle, extinguishing the glow that provided light inside the house.

"Out of my way! Out of my way!" Shack yelled as he barreled through the doorway. He hit the corner of the makeshift plywood door, knocking it and Ben to the ground.

"You're in my way, idiot." Shack placed both of his meaty hands on Ben's shoulders and lifted his body up. Ben could smell honey barbeque on Shack's breath.

Ben got up, and the trio hurried back down the path and disappeared into the night. Rian, Wayne, Luis, and Hassan remained frozen in place and waited for someone to signal that it was safe to move.

20

THE STASH

When she figured it was safe, Rian finally came out from around the side of the house. She walked to the bush and helped Wayne to his feet. He was covered in leaves and thorns. Hassan and Luis came out from their hiding place in the dark woods and joined the others.

After taking a moment to appreciate how close they had just come to certain death, they crept into the house and stood in the center of the kitchen. It was pitch black except for a hint of moonlight that made the faintest glow of blue light in the back corner of the room.

Rian got on her hands and knees and crept around looking for the candle Shack had kicked over earlier. Floundering around, she reached out and grabbed Wayne's ankle, causing him to jump. Eventually she felt the hardened, freshly cooled wax spilled out across the floor. Using that as a guide, her hand eventually landed on the candle.

The candle was useless without something to light it. She remembered Shack and Janessa smoking cigarettes. The smell still lingered in the air.

They must have left a lighter somewhere in the room she thought to herself. Rian moved to the moonlit corner of the kitchen and motioned for her friends to come to her.

She showed the boys the candle, and pretended to light it with an imaginary lighter. *Search*, she urged her friends with her hand cupped around her eye.

Their eyes adjusted to the dark as they scoured the room for something to light the candle. Hassan's foot kicked the plastic Wawa bag and everything left inside of it. He picked it up and reached in.

There it was! A cigarette lighter. It took him four attempts at turning the spark wheel, but eventually he got it lit!

Awesome! Wayne signed with his palms in the air.

Hassan lit the candle, and they looked around the room. Every inch of the kitchen proved that the house was a shell of its former self. Green wooden cabinets were bare, most no longer having doors to conceal that fact. Sheets of vinyl flooring that curled at the corners exposed the warped and rotted subfloor below, damaged from years of rain that seeped in through a giant hole in the ceiling. Pink floral wallpaper peeled off in sheets and exposed broken plaster and wood lath slats like a rib cage unmasked from a covering of skin and muscle.

A few random kitchen items sat abandoned on the counter. A mixing bowl, a fork, three spoons, and a broken coffee mug with the words 'My Pops is Tops' written across the front. The recently heaved piece of mortar sat beside the mug.

A cast iron sink sat on the floor next to an empty pantry with no door. Sticking out of the wall was a drain pipe and a pair of severed water lines once connected to the sink.

This-place-is cool! signed Luis.

Hassan and Wayne seemed equally impressed with the kitchen, but Rian did not like it at all. It scared her. "Let's get out of here," she said, heading toward the door.

"You still scared." Hassan taunted her.

Luis laughed and signed, *Ghost*, pinching his index finger and thumb on both hands and pulling away as if he were unfurling a string.

"Lou say you scared of a ghost," said Hassan.

"I don't like this place," Rian shot back. The intensity on her face said back off, and so they did. They were not about to leave, but they did not tease Rian again.

They searched the kitchen, or what was left of it, opening drawers and peeking in the pantry, looking for anything interesting. Hassan came to a large oven with silver knobs jutting out of the front. He grasped a long metal bar on the oven door and slowly started to pull it open.

"Don't," Rian yelled. "There might be an animal living in there."

The warning caused Hassan to pause. He shut the door, and with the palm of his hand he wiped decades of dirt and grease off a small glass plate on the front and peeked inside.

"I see something," he said, curiously.

His intrigue required action. Grabbing the handle of the oven once again, Hassan yanked the door open hard. As he pulled it open, he jumped back, making sure if an animal did jump out it would not land on him.

There was no animal, but the oven wasn't empty. It contained a trove of stuff that was too new to belong to the house. Inside the oven sat a stuffed penguin, a pencil box, an old cell phone, hats and gloves, a Rubik's Cube, a pack of baseball cards, a pair of pink flip flops, and even a brown leather cigarette case made of crunched leather with a metal clasp at the top.

They looked at each other confused. Digging deeper, they found a stack of books in the back of the oven.

"Look," Hassan yelled. He moved a few things to the side and pulled out a large red book with a white spiral binding. The cover of the book had a picture of a lion in spectacles sitting at a table adjacent to a giraffe wearing a necktie. Across the top of the book in all capital letters was the word 'Highways.'

"Bae-Hue's book!" Hassan said. "Shack steal it!"

Luis whipped his hand briskly into a fist as if snatching the air in front of him and pointed at the items in the oven.

Let's-take it! he signed excitedly.

141

Wayne and Luis grabbed the stash and laid everything out on the counter.

"If we take it, Shack knows we were here," Hassan countered.

He-won't know-it was us, Luis signed.

Wayne pressed the power button on the cell phone, and the bright white LED light shone on his face.

"I got the phone," said Wayne.

"That's stealing," said Rian.

"It's already stolen," said Wayne defiantly.

Without warning, Luis snatched the phone out of Wayne's grasp.

Mine, he signed, pressing his open palm to his chest.

"Shack, stole your phone? We need to steal him!" Wayne insisted.

"What is that supposed to mean?" Rian asked.

"It means we hit him, hard," Wayne replied.

"Maybe we give it all back," said Hassan.

"To who?" Wayne replied.

Hassan picked up the *Highways* teacher's edition and said, "Bae-Hue!"

Wayne picked up the big red book and tossed it back into the oven. "Forget that thing," he said.

Rian got up and one by one started returning the stash of items back to the oven.

"We need tell Bae-Hue what Shack does," said Hassan.

Luis answered back, his finger shooting out across his chin.

Snitch! he signed disgustedly.

"Shack steal all this," Hassan replied.

Luis shook his head and fingerspelled, *So what?*

"None of us are taking this stuff. We know it's here. Let's see if we can figure out who these things belong to, and then we'll figure out what to do with it. Right now, Shack doesn't know anyone was here. If we take this stuff, he will figure it out," answered Rian.

Luis held up his cellphone and once again slapped his chest over and over insisting the device was his. There was no doubt, it wasn't going back in the oven.

"Keep your phone. Everything else goes back," said Rian.

Reluctantly, Wayne and the others agreed. They placed everything back in the oven.

When they were finished, Wayne closed the oven door, and a cold rush of wind filled the room, extinguishing the candle that sat on the edge of the counter. They were once again in total darkness.

"What happened?" Rian asked out loud.

They fumbled around the room for a couple of minutes before Luis made his way to the exit and left the house. Hassan and Wayne followed. Rian was on her way out of the back door when she felt someone watching her. Turning around, she saw a figure standing at the end of the hallway at the opposite side of the house. In that moment, it looked as though two glowing red eyes were peering at her.

Frightened, she bolted out of the house and ran into Wayne. "What's your problem?" he asked.

Rian just shook her head and looked at the others.

"We need to go," she said. "We're late!"

21

BIRTHDAY SURPRISE

The chill in the air gave notice that November was in full swing. That morning, Rian was awakened to the smell of pumpkin soup coming from the kitchen. She followed the smell and found Joanna standing over the stove pouring coconut milk into a red pot. Rian hated Joanna's pumpkin soup, but she made the mistake a few years back of telling her that she loved it, to spare her feelings, and now it was part of the regular rotation on the fall menu.

Rian had been grounded since coming home late Halloween night. She got home around 9:30 and was surprised that her mother was not angry with her. Joanna had been terrified and then elated when Rian returned home unharmed. It was Aunt Nancy who was furious with her. She felt she had gone out on a limb to make the case that Rian was responsible enough to be trusted, and in so doing, Rian made her look like a fool.

The punishment hardly fit the crime. Since none of Rian's friends actually lived in Millbrook Park, being told she had to stay home was not much different than her usual routine. She was not allowed to use electronics either, but TV was not at all interesting to her, she wasn't a gamer, and she didn't own a phone. Basically, her punishment boiled down to not being allowed to look at YouTube on Joanna's laptop for a week.

As Joanna made her soup, Rian sat at the kitchen table working on a portrait of her father. Her favorite photo of him, a picture taken two years earlier in Wildwood, was paper-clipped to the top of one page, and her portrait was coming to life on the other. The picture was a gift for her dad.

144

She could not wait to finally see him again and get out of Millbrook Park, even if only for a weekend.

She was having a tough time drawing his eyes. They were either too far apart, or not in the right place, or the wrong shape. If the eyes were wrong, the picture was wrong, and she needed her father to love this picture. It meant everything to her.

Her birthday was coming up, and she was planning to spend the weekend at his apartment. She was so excited to see him. Between his busy work schedule and all the time he spent with his new girlfriend, Elizabeth, and her kids, Rian hadn't seen much of him since moving to Millbrook Park.

She was not thrilled to spend her birthday with his girlfriend and her kids, but it was the price to pay to finally spend some quality time with him, and she was willing to pay it.

"You want a taste? Pumpkin soup!" Joanna's inflection rose with each word, crescendoing on the word soup, implying a shared excitement about it.

Joanna recently found a new job answering calls at a local veterinary clinic. Her shift didn't start for a few hours so she was spending the morning cheerily making her soup.

Rian smiled half-heartedly. "Maybe later," she said with a forced smile.

"Two more days until your birthday!" Joanna said excitedly. "I was thinking we should plan a birthday party."

Rian had no interest in planning a birthday party. She was focused on seeing her dad and spending the weekend in her old neighborhood. If anything, she wanted a party there and a chance to see her old friends.

"That's okay," Rian said.

"You're going to be twelve years old. We have to do something to celebrate," she insisted.

"What time is Dad coming to pick me up?" Rian asked.

"How about ice skating? You love ice skating. There's a place not far from here. I checked and they have three hour birthday party packages," Joanna insisted.

"I don't need a party, Mom," said Rian. "Besides, I'll be with Dad for my birthday, so the party wouldn't be until next weekend. My birthday will be passed by then. It's no big deal."

"Of course it's a big deal. You only turn twelve once," said Joanna.

"Does this mean I'm not grounded?" Rian asked.

Caught off guard by the question, Joanna responded, "Yeah, yes. Of course. You've served your time."

"Well, I guess it could be fun," said Rian.

"Great, I'll call the ice rink," said Joanna.

"Actually, could we do a bowling party?" Rian asked.

"Bowling? I didn't know you liked to bowl." Said Joanna.

"Well, my friends talk about it a lot, and if I'm going to party with my Millbrook friends, then that's what I want to do. Go bowling."

Joanna's face soured.

"Your friends? You don't mean those boys you went trick-or-treating with the other night? Ri, I don't know if I want you spending time with those boys," she said.

"You just said you wanted me to have a birthday party with my friends," said Rian.

"Not those friends. Why don't we invite your hearing friends," replied Joanna.

"I have one friend at Hancock who isn't deaf," said Rian.

"Okay, that's a start," said Joanna.

"And she has one arm," said Rian.

146

Joanna dropped the wooden spoon she was using to stir the soup into the pot.

"Ri, I think it's nice that you are trying to reach out to the disabled kids at your school…"

"Disabled?" Rian yelled. "They're not disabled. They're different, not disabled."

"I didn't mean it like that. It's great that you're their friend and that I raised a daughter who can see past people's limitations, but don't you think you should try to make some other friends too?" Joanna asked.

"I've tried, Mom," Rian wasn't yelling but still speaking loudly. Her voice cracked a bit, giving away her frustration over this conversation. "These are the kids who like me. And I like them. If I can't invite them to my party, then I don't want a party!"

Joanna moved the pot off the burner to allow it to cool. She grabbed a towel off the front of the oven and wiped creamy orange droplets from the cooktop as she spoke.

"I have an idea. Why don't we just invite the entire class? That way your friends can come, and maybe you can make some new friends too."

Rian's face had turned red as she fought back tears. The conversation was making her very upset. At that moment, Nancy entered the kitchen. She recognized Rian's sad expression and turned to Joanna.

"You told her?" she asked Joanna who was shaking her head back and forth and shooting a wide-eyed look directly at her sister. "I'm sorry, kiddo. Your mom and I talked about it, and we are going to do whatever you want to celebrate your birthday this weekend."

"What are you talking about?" asked Rian. "I'm going with Dad this weekend."

Nancy turned white as she turned back to Joanna. Joanna abandoned the soup and stepped toward Rian.

"Sweetheart…" Joanna was immediately interrupted.

"Nope. Whatever you're thinking of saying, don't say it. Dad is coming. He promised he is coming."

"Baby, he called last night…" again she was interrupted.

"I'm going upstairs. I have to finish packing." Rian abruptly turned and ran out of the kitchen.

Joanna found Rian sitting on her bed working on her father's portrait. She was darkening the shadows on his cheek when she heard Joanna step toward her. She arched her back so as to bury her face and block the picture with her body.

Joanna sat next to Rian on the bed.

"We're not talking about this," said Rian.

"He called last night. He was very upset about it, but he's stuck in Vegas for another week working on a project. He promised he will call you later. He's planning to reschedule…"

Teardrops plunked onto the portrait as Joanna spoke. Rian shuffled the picture to the other side of the bed and wiped her cheeks.

"We're fighters. You and I. I know this hurts, but you're a tough kid. All of this has been difficult for you, and it's not fair. All I can say is I'm sorry, baby," said Joanna.

"I hate this place. I hate Millbrook Park. I hate Hancock. I want to go home," Rian said.

"I know this isn't where we thought we'd be. Sometimes life just hands you a big bowl of lemons. You just have to make the best of it," said Joanna.

"The best of it?" Rian's voice increased in intensity. "Why do I have to make the best of it? It wasn't my choice to leave home. It was yours! I don't understand why you and Dad had to get a divorce anyway. He didn't move into the city. Why did we?"

148

"Life isn't always what we expect. Do you think I planned this? You think I wanted to divorce your father and move here?"

"Well, you did, and here we are." Rian's fists were balled up at her side.

"Did it ever occur to you that maybe it isn't all my fault? That maybe your father had something to do with it?"

"Of course you blame him. He isn't here to defend himself," Rian yelled at Joanna.

"No, he's not here to defend himself. He's too busy with Elizabeth and her kids to care what either of us is doing. Well, I'm here, and I'm sorry if you don't like it, but you're stuck with me. Just me. So if you think that sucks then I guess it sucks, but it's not going to change."

"Get out!" Rian shot up and pointed at the door as she yelled at her mother.

Joanna realized she lost her temper, and her words had just made the situation much worse. The genie was out of the bottle, and there was no putting it back.

"I'm sorry, Rian," Joanna said softly. "I didn't mean…"

"Get out," Rian stormed to the door and grabbed the knob.

Joanna got up, now needing to wipe the tears away from her own eyes. She walked out the door, and Rian slammed it behind her. Falling forward, she collapsed on her bed and cried for the rest of the morning.

22

THUNDERBIRD LANES

👌🤙👋👆🤟✊👐✊👇👌 ✊🤙👐👆👍

After a few days of feeling sorry for herself, Rian decided she wanted a party after all. A last-minute cancelation at Thunderbird Lanes gave Joanna the opportunity to reserve four lanes and a party room to celebrate Rian's birthday.

She was feeling much better after Joanna gave her the big gift: a cell phone of her own. Her actual birthday fell on a Wednesday, and so by Saturday she had forgotten all about the disappointment of not going to Penn Hills to see her dad.

Four available lanes were enough to invite everyone in her class, with two notable exceptions. Shack and Ben Ellis were left off the guest list. With only a few days to respond about half of the class showed up to the party. Among the attendees were Lucas, Elisha, Jamilah, Reg Mosely, Evander Burton, Samantha Tenny, Gavin Ruthledge, Haroon Jacobs, Luis, Hassan, Wayne and Sandra.

Luis was nervous about going to the party. He didn't mention to his mother that Rian was a girl and not just any girl. She was the girl he had met at the mall with the cochlear implant. At first he hoped his father would bring him to the party. His dad didn't much care one way or the other about any of Luis's friends so long as he stayed out of trouble, but it was his mother who brought him, not his father.

As they entered the bowling alley, Luis could feel a lump growing in his throat. He should have just told Jennifer the truth about Rian earlier. He pushed the thought aside, knowing she would have said no to the party altogether. He was not going to miss this party. Not only was it a bowling party, he knew Sandra would be there.

Luis and Jennifer were the last to arrive. They drifted past the lanes along the pink and purple carpeted alley until they came to an area marked "Party Rooms." They saw the words "Happy Birthday Rian" written on a dry erase board outside the doorway, so they entered that room.

The small room had cinder block walls painted in purple hues that matched the rest of the alley. A white, plastic tablecloth with a playful design of balloons and confetti was draped over three rickety tables. A pink frosted cake sprouting twelve candles was neatly placed before a metal folding chair at the head of the table. A balloon with a smiling yellow-faced emoji was tied to the folding chair of honor.

Joanna was pouring chips into a plastic bowl when Jennifer and Luis entered the room. Jennifer nudged Luis to put the present he was holding on a small table in the corner that was lined with gift bags and envelopes.

As Luis put the present on the table, Joanna turned to greet her guest but hesitated when she saw Luis. She flashed a nervous smile his way.

Jennifer walked over and held out her hand to shake Joanna's. Feeling silly, Joanna clasped Jennifer's hand and spoke.

"Hi, I'm Joanna," she could see right away that Jennifer did not understand Joanna.

"I'm Jo-an-na," she repeated, this time much more loudly, breaking her name into over-pronounced syllables.

Luis introduced Joanna as *Rian's-mom*, using the name sign with the twisting R running from his head to his shoulder. Until now, he fingerspelled her name, fully aware his mother would recognize the name sign as belonging to the girl he met at the mall.

With a look of surprise, Jennifer repeated the sign to make sure she understood him. Luis anxiously nodded to confirm.

"You must be Luis's mom. I'm so happy you could make it. It's nice to meet you, I'm Joanna," Joanna said loudly, over pronouncing each syllable

151

of each word. Her speech had the effect of making her facial expressions unnatural and silly. Jennifer resisted the urge to chuckle.

Jennifer reached into her handbag and grabbed her cellphone. She opened the magnetic clasp of the pink leather case, turned it on and searched for an app called Live Caption. Live Caption was an app that she used anytime she was in a situation that required her to communicate with hearing people.

"Luis, you made it!" Rian said, running into the room and shattering the silence. She was followed closely behind by Sandra.

Excited to see Sandra, Luis smiled and pointed to Jennifer and signed, *My-mom*.

Rian froze when she saw Jennifer. Her mind flashed to that day at the mall and the look on Jennifer's face when she signed that word. *Implant*. Undaunted, Rian was prepared for this moment. She had practiced what she would say to Jennifer earlier that week. With her sign language dictionary in hand, she had looked up signs and prepared things to say, to show Jennifer she could be Deaf too.

Nice-to meet-you, Rian said, signing the words slowly and methodically to avoid making a mistake. *I am-Rian*.

Recognizing Rian's attempt to communicate with her in sign, Jennifer turned off her phone, closed the leather case and slipped it back into her bag. She was curious to see just how well this girl could sign.

Nice-to meet-you, Jennifer smiled as she returned the greeting. *Happy-Birthday!*

Rian was immediately confused. The first thing she looked up in her dictionary was the phrase *happy birthday*. She recognized *happy*, that was easy, but Joanna signed *birthday* by tugging on her earlobe. That was not the sign Rian knew for *birthday*. Rian thought Jennifer would sign the word by touching her chin and her heart with bent middle finger.

Was that happy birthday? She wondered. *Should I say thank you and risk looking dumb if that isn't what she said? Should I ask her to repeat?*

"Let's go!" Sandra said, grabbing Luis by the hand and turning to leave.

They ran out of the room together. Rian decided to abandon her plan to impress Jennifer with her ability to sign. Defeated, she followed behind Luis and Sandra but was stopped by Joanna.

"Wait, Ri, introduce me to Luis's mother please," she said.

"But I want to join my friends," Rian spoke and didn't sign. She knew that was rude, but she was preoccupied with getting out of there as fast as possible.

"Just for a minute. Don't be rude," Joanna insisted.

Taking a deep breath and turning back to Jennifer, Rian pointed to Joanna and signed, *My-mom, J-O-A-N-N-A.*

After fingerspelling her name, Jennifer put her finger to her cheek and twisted it just a bit. "Jennifer," she said clearly enough to understand, surprising Joanna and Rian.

Do you-have-a name-sign? Jennifer asked Joanna.

"What did she ask?" asked Joanna.

"I think she asked if you have a name sign?" said Rian, turning and repeating the words *name* and *sign* to Jennifer.

"What's a name sign?" asked Joanna.

Rian turned back to Jennifer and signed the letter J by her chin, brushing her pinky lightly against the corner of her mouth. She proudly said, "Joanna."

Who-gave her-that name-sign? Jennifer asked.

Rian pointed to herself proudly and repeated it. Then she explained, *Because-she is-my-mom.*

Jennifer was not impressed. She did not consider Rian a true member of the Deaf community, and only true members of the Deaf community are allowed to give a person a name sign.

Jennifer shook her head and waved off the sign name. To be clear, she fingerspelled Joanna's name to Rian, to make sure she understood correctly, and then she gave Joanna a new name sign. This time she drew and imaginary *J* in the air, in front of her mouth. It was a slight adjustment, with a bigger purpose.

Jennifer explained the change by signing, *Because-she's-hearing-like-you.*

Rian understood exactly what Jennifer was trying to say. She recognized the sign for *hearing*, the index finger rolling in circles in front of Jennifer's mouth.

"Rian, are you going to tell me what you two are talking about? You're not saying anything," said Joanna.

"Mrs. Rodriguez gave you a new name sign," Rian said, repeating it for her mother. She did not mention that Jennifer called her hearing. In her life, she had been called many things, deaf, hard of hearing, a CI, but this was the first time anyone called her hearing. For some reason, being called it felt like an insult.

"Rian, ask her where she lives," Joanna said, with excitement in her voice.

"Mom, I want to get back to my friends," Rian said desperately.

"Go on, ask her where she lives," Joanna insisted.

Hesitantly, Rian turned to Joanna and wagged her index finger back and forth to ask, *Where?*

Rian tensed up. Her plan to show Jennifer her signing skills was quickly falling apart. Now she couldn't even sign something as simple as this. She knew the sign for *live,* but her mind went blank. She stood stupidly, staring at Jennifer, desperately trying to remember the sign. Jennifer stood patiently waiting for Rian to finish her question.

Suddenly, it came to her.

Live, she signed running her left and right hands, with *L* handshapes from her waist to her chest.

When Jennifer signed with hearing people, it was usually with an interpreter. Some interpreters were fine people and others bothered her. It especially bothered her when she would worked with an interpreter who initialized their signs.

Initializing, simply explained, is when a sign has been modified from its original ASL form by using a handshape that represents the first letter of the word being used. It was a pet peeve for Jennifer who considered herself to use pure ASL and rarely initialized words.

Jennifer repeated Rian's way of signing *live* with *L* handshapes and shook her head disapprovingly. She then signed *live* once again, this time with closed fists, showing Rian the ASL way to sign the word.

She was not sure if Rian understood her point, but she could see that Rian was embarrassed. Feeling badly, Jennifer changed her demeanor and answered the question.

R-H-A-W-N-H-U-R-S-T, she slowly fingerspelled the name of her neighborhood.

Rian was relieved. She knew Luis lived in Rhawnhurst, so Jennifer's fingerspelled answer was easy for her to understand.

"Rhawnhurst," she proudly announced to Joanna.

"Wow. Tell her I said that's really far. Oh, then tell her I am happy she and Luis could come," Joanna said, still speaking very loudly and slowly. In the excitement of the moment, she was now moving her arms and gesturing too.

"You don't have to talk like that mom," Rian said.

"Like what?" Joanna asked, offended.

"Never mind," answered Rian.

Looking back to Jennifer, Rian considered her mother's words for a moment before trying to translate.

Rian signed *happy* and *come*, but she didn't know the sign for the word *far*, so she skipped it. She wasn't using her voice, so her mother had no idea what she was saying anyway.

"Ask her if she wants something to eat or drink?" insisted Joanna.

Rian asked, and Jennifer politely declined.

"Rian, tell her we have pizza and hot dogs," said Joanna.

"She just said she didn't want any," said Rian.

"Go on, Rian. Ask her if she would like pizza or a hot dog," Joanna insisted, frustrating Rian.

Eat? Rian signed with an inquisitive look. *Pizza-hot-dog*, she signed dog and hot as separate words, unaware that she had just asked Jennifer if she wanted to devour an overheated canine.

This time, Jennifer couldn't help but laugh a little. She walked over to the crock pot, and with a pair of tongs she removed a hot dog and placed it in a bun.

Hot dog, she signed, balling her fists two times across her body. Then she took a bite and signed, *Thank you.*

"Now tell her we have soda and water…" Joanna's request was interrupted after Jennifer placed her hot dog on the table and waved her hand to get Joanna's attention.

Talk to-me-please, Jennifer signed.

Turning to Rian, Joanna asked, "What did she say?"

"She wants you to talk to her," Rian growled, frustrated and embarrassed.

"I am speaking to her," Joanna said directly to Rian.

"No, you're talking to me. Ask her the questions, and I will sign what you ask," Rian said, wanting to crawl under the table and hide.

"Is that rude? Oh, tell her I'm sorry," said Joanna.

"Just say, sorry!" huffed Rian.

"I'm sorry," Joanna said, finally looking Jennifer in the eye.

Fine, Jennifer signed to reassure them, placing her thumb in the center of her chest. Changing the topic, Jennifer placed her hand to her forehead and asked Rian, *Is your-father-here?*

Rian recognized the sign for father and filled in the rest. She shook her head no. Earlier in the week, Luis taught her the sign for *divorce.* She was explaining why she was upset with her mom and had asked him because she was tired of fingerspelling it.

My parents-are divorced, Rian signed, surprising Jennifer.

Jennifer repeated the signs reversing their order. Her face showed both concern and curiosity.

Sorry, she signed moving her eyes from Rian to Joanna.

"What are you talking about?" Joanna asked.

"School. I said I like it," Rian said, lying once again.

Feeling like a complete fool, Rian turned to her mother and asked, "Can I please get back to bowling? They're going to start without me."

Joanna agreed, and Rian thanked Jennifer once again and bolted out the door, leaving the two moms in the room alone. Joanna reached down and lifted a red plastic cup filled with cola. She smiled and then drank the contents of the cup. Jennifer returned to her hot dog.

Joanna left the cup in front of her mouth, as if she were hiding behind it. She turned away from Jennifer and waited anxiously for another adult to enter the room.

A little while later, Rian was having a blast at the party. Sandra, Luis, Hassan, and she shared a lane and had set up a friendly, boys versus girls competition. The boys had won the first two games and were well ahead early in the third. Everything was going well until Francisco and Alex, two Deaf friends of Luis's showed up.

They hadn't yet gotten their bowling shoes when they saw Luis and came over to say hello. They held up the game for ten minutes. Eventually Sandra told Luis that she was tired of waiting for him to take his turn. Francisco and Alex were surprised by Sandra's interruption into their conversation since Luis hadn't bothered to introduce anyone. Both took immediate notice of Sandra's arm.

Your-friend? Francisco signed to Luis with an expression of amusement that wasn't lost on Sandra.

"Yeah, we friends," she said, signing the word *friend* aggressively. "Who is you?"

Luis pointed to Sandra and signed her name, then he pointed to Hassan and Wayne and signed their names. He gestured for them to come over for a proper introduction. It led to another ten minute delay of the game.

Rian was annoyed. Luis was holding up the game because of these two boys who showed up at her party, and to make matters worse, he didn't even bother to introduce her to them. She wanted to finish the game before cake and ice cream, so Rian decided to introduce herself to Francisco and Alex and politely request Luis and the others get back to bowling.

"Hi, I'm Rian," she said, signing her name and reaching out for a handshake as she walked over.

Alex turned to Luis with a quizzical look. Not a word was spoken or signed, but Rian read that look as easily as she read the words *Snack Bar* printed in bright red letters over the counter behind them.

He's judging me. He doesn't know anything about me, except that I have a cochlear implant, and he's already judging me, she thought to herself.

Wanting to be the bigger person, Rian ignored the look and signed, *Nice-to meet-you.*

Francisco and Alex nodded and limply waved at her, then turned their attention back to Luis. And Hassan. And Wayne. Her frustration grew. What was happening? Hassan and Wayne were now BFFs with these party crashers too?

Rian walked over to Sandra who had given up on Francisco and Alex and was on her phone.

"Who are these bozos?" Rian asked sarcastically.

Sandra looked up from her phone and said matter-of-factly, "That's Francisco and Alex."

Even Sandra didn't seem to care.

I must be the only person who notices how rude this behavior is. Does no one else even care that we are celebrating my birthday, Rian thought to herself.

"Hey girl!" Elisha said as she passed the group and headed toward the snack bar.

"Hi Elisha," Rian called back.

Having had enough, Rian decided it was time to reclaim her party. She waved her hands to get Luis attention, but he acted like he did not see her. Growing more frustrated by the minute, Rian stepped between Luis and Francisco blocking them from continuing their conversation.

Ready? she signed to Luis.

Her one word request made Francisco and Alex laugh out loud. Alex pretended he had a whip and that he was cracking it in Luis direction.

Luis, clearly embarrassed, rolls his eyes and turned back to Francisco and Alex. He performed a choreographed hand shake with each boy that took another three minutes to complete, and finally returned to the to finish bowling.

Rian tried to forget the incident and get back to having fun, but the damage had been done. Luis's attitude had clearly changed. He tossed the ball on his turn and didn't speak between frames. He looked both embarrassed and annoyed.

When bowling was over, the guests gathered in the party room as Joanna served the pizza, hot dogs, and soda. Rian was thrilled when Elisha sat to her right at the head of table. Sandra was to her left, and she was once again enjoying the party.

When it was time to cut the cake, Rian noticed that Luis and Hassan were not in the room. She asked Joanna to hold off for just a minute so she could gather the boys.

Leaving the room, she saw Luis and Hassan with Francisco and Alex in lane seventeen. They weren't just hanging out, their names had been added to the digital scoreboard over the lane. Surprised, and more than a little offended, Rian put her feelings in check and headed over to let them know it was time to cut the cake.

Luis saw Rian heading toward them. She gestured for them to come back as she headed over. Luis turned away, pretending not to notice, but it was clear he saw her.

He got up and hurried over to the ball return. He sank his fingers into a candy-apple red ball with white marbling all around it and swiped it out of the tray. Without hesitation, he walked to the line and stopped.

The ball rested in his hands just inches from his nose, but his mind was focused on Rian. He refused to look back, hoping she had turned around and went back to the party room. Unable to resist the urge, he turned back ever so slightly and saw Rian standing next to Francisco.

Cake! She signed emphatically, noticing that he finally turned her way.

Francisco repeated Rian's sign, behind her back, and the enthusiasm she used to convey the message. Furious that she wouldn't leave him alone, Luis turned his eyes to the ten bowling pins before him, cocked back and launched the ball down the lane. It soared through the air and hit the wood hard, veered to the left and slammed into the gulley alongside the wooden runway.

Luis's terrible throw caused everyone to laugh, Francisco, Alex, Hassan, and Rian. Luis was not amused.

He stomped over to Rian, and with big exaggerated movements he signed, *I don't want-cake.*

Trying to save face, Rian then signed, *We-have-ice cream-to.*

Unfortunately, Rian signed the directional word, *to,* pointing one index finger to the tip of the other instead of the adverb, *too,* meaning also.

The mistake provided even more reason for Francisco and Alex to laugh at Rian's expense. Luis buried his face in his hands and shook his head in disbelief.

Go back to-the party! Leave-us alone! Luis signed as Hassan apologetically voiced for his friend.

Fine, Rian said, before turning and storming off. Her eyes welled with tears, and the closer she got to the room the slower she approached. She did not want her guests to see her crying. Her mom came to the doorway to see what was happening.

Rian turned away, back toward Luis and the other boys. She could see them making fun of her. Although she didn't understand most of what they were signing, there was one sign she recognized clearly. It was the sign Luis had used as an insult the day they met. It was the sign his mother used with a look of disgust that day at the mall.

Rian watched them put their bent fingers behind their ears, like vampire teeth sinking deep into flesh. Now, it was she that was suddenly filled with rage. She thought that she and Luis were past this. She thought they were friends and that he saw her as a Deaf person like him. She was wrong. At the first opportunity to disavow her to other Deaf friends, Luis jumped at the chance.

How could he do this to her? He was ruining her birthday.

Without giving it a second thought, Rian stormed back to the bowling lane and walked right up to Luis.

Although he did feel bad for his behavior, he kept up his front.

What-do you-want? He signed with an exasperated look on his face.

Rian didn't know what to say. She was hurt. She was sad, and most of all, she was angry. Luis, Hassan, Francisco and Alex anxiously waited for her to say something.

Asshole! she blurted out, hurling the sign directly at Luis.

Francisco and Alex fell over laughing. Hassan's eyes were huge, and Luis's mouth hit the floor. Feeling she had made her point Rian turned and ran out of Thunderbird Lanes, completely abandoning the party.

23

FIGHT

Rian sat with her back against the large curved outer wall of the school. She had her sketch pad out, and she was drawing a picture of her old house. Specifically, she was drawing the old maple tree in her front yard. She had finished the blue house with the red door, and although there was no color in the drawing, the hues were vibrant in her mind.

"We going to the movies Saturday. You coming?" asked Sandra, who was sitting beside Rian.

"No, I've got things to do," Rian answered, without taking her eyes off her drawing.

"You drawlin'," said Sandra.

Rian took her pencil off the page, turned the book to show Sandra her drawing and said, "Yeah, it's a picture of my old house."

"I didn't say draw-ing," Sandra overemphasized the last syllable of the last word to make a point. I said you drawlin'. You outta pocket," Sandra continued.

Rian placed the sketch pad on the ground beside her and turned to Sandra and asked, "You want me to forgive Luis? Forget it! You were there, you saw how he ruined my birthday."

"He's sorry. Really. He feels bad about all that. Can't you forgive him already? It's been two weeks," exclaimed Sandra.

"He hasn't asked for forgiveness. He hasn't even tried to talk to me since the party," said Rian.

"I'll get him," Sandra said, rising to her feet.

"No. Don't. I don't want to talk to him," exclaimed Rian.

"This whole thing is dumb. Ya'll need to work it out," said Sandra.

"If he wants to say he's sorry, I guess I am ready to listen," said Rian.

She watched Sandra run off to find Luis. Her attention moved from Sandra to the rest of the school yard. Nathan and Antoine led a game of kickball. There must have been twenty kids playing. Lucas played a card game with Dan Donnelly, a boy from Mr. Herman's homeroom. Elisha and Jamilah had their phones out and were actively ignoring one another. Rian's eyes settled on Shack.

He had Ben Ellis in a headlock and was galloping around in a circle with Ben's head tucked neatly under his arm. Ben made no effort to resist. The ride ended when a recess aide came over and blew her whistle. While Shack pleaded his case, Ben ran off to play kickball.

Rian returned to her picture. Studying it, she felt something was missing. The feeling caused a sense of despair. She had moved away at the end of the summer, and already the place was disappearing from her memory. What was missing? She stared and stared but couldn't figure it out.

She peered over her sketch pad once again and saw Shack lumbering her way. His arms swung from side to side like a slow-moving gorilla. She looked back down at her sketch pad and tried to hide behind the pages. Her eyes were fixed on the maple tree in the drawing, and she imagined herself climbing up the trunk and hiding in its branches.

He doesn't see me, she thought to herself. *He has other things to do.*

She wanted to peer over the sketch pad again, just for a second, to make sure he wasn't heading her way. Just a second to confirm he had found someone else to torment. Her eyes looked up over the book.

He was standing right in front of her. She quickly went back to drawing.

Maybe he isn't here to bother me. If I look busy, he might just walk right past me. Wasn't recess almost over, anyway? Rian tried to convince herself.

"What's up, magnet head? Your jawn's still broken? That sucks," Shack laughed as he spoke, his words pinning her back to the wall.

Rian pretended not to hear him. She lifted her pencil to the book and suddenly remembered what she had forgotten; the flagstone walkway. Her hand trembled as she added it to her drawing.

Without warning, Shack snatched the sketch pad out of her hand. A familiar sense of helplessness came over her. The same feeling that struck when he took her implants on her first day of school. It was as if he tore a limb from her body.

Not my drawings. Please don't hurt my book! Rian thought to herself, hearing her voice scream out in her head.

Shack stared at her drawing. A smile crossed his face as he admired it. It was as if he were studying it. Rian didn't want him to study the house. It was her house and her picture.

"Not bad. What else you got?" he asked, aggressively thumbing through the book. "Wow, look at this one."

Shack turned the sketch pad around and held up the portrait of her father.

"This is your dad?" he asked.

"Yes," she said nervously. She wasn't sure what to make of this conversation.

"He's deaf like you?" Shack asked.

"No," said Rian.

"You don't have to be embarrassed. I think he is deaf. These things run in families. That's how it works, right? You're deaf because others in your family are deaf?"

"I am the only person in my family with hearing loss, besides my grandfather. He's just old," she forced a laugh hoping he might laugh back.

165

He did not. Instead, he bent over and took the pencil out of her hand.

"Let's make him deaf," Shack said, putting the pencil to the paper and running over the page in circles.

She couldn't speak as she watched this ogre draw over the portrait. She thought about trying to grab it from him but knew she would fail. She decided to let him do whatever he was going to do to the picture and hope it would end there. If she was lucky, destroying the portrait was all he had time for.

Is the bell ever going to ring? She thought to herself.

"There," he said. "Much better. Now he's deaf like you."

Shack turned the sketch pad around to show off the changes he made to her drawing. There were large black swirling circles in her father's ears with a line, like a wire, connecting the shapes. He drew over her father's eyes and replaced them with a new set of sloppily drawn crossed eyes. A hastily drawn tongue protruded unnaturally from his mouth, and a speech bubble with the words *I'm def* filled the top left corner of the page.

"What do you think?" asked Shack.

"Can I have it back now?" she asked.

"I'm a fan of your work," Shack flipped through the sketch pad as he spoke. "I might be your biggest fan, actually. I'm going to keep this, I think."

Shack tucked the sketch pad under his arm. Neither he nor Rian noticed Sandra and Luis approaching. As he turned to leave he saw them standing in his way.

"What do you want?" Shack asked dismissively.

"Give it back!" Sandra demanded.

"This?" Shack asked, reaching under his arm to grasp the sketch pad. "She gave it to me. I'm her biggest fan."

"Give it back, or else Luis is gonna take it back," Sandra pushed Luis, moving him closer to Shack.

What? Luis signed to Sandra, unsure what she was saying but certain it was going to get him in trouble.

"I said ya'll gonna fight this boul unless he gives Rian back her drawings," Sandra said, signing *Fight* by brushing her left fist over the end of her limb.

"Is that right?" Shack asked, stepping toward Luis, his tall frame casting a shadow as he glared down at him.

Luis's eyes turned to Sandra. How could she do this to him? She couldn't possibly think he would be able to fight Shack and survive. Acting tough, he glared at Shack but said nothing.

"You're planning to take this?" he asked, holding the book out, daring Luis to grab it. "Go on. Take it."

Luis lunged to grab the sketch pad but missed as Shack pulled it back toward his body. Shack laughed at the half-hearted attempt by Luis.

"Yo, do something," Sandra urged Luis.

"Yeah, do something," Shack repeated.

"Back!" Luis spoke the command clearly enough for the all to understand.

"I told you, she gave it to me," said Shack.

"Back!" Luis said again, taking a step toward Shack.

Shack leaned in, only inches from Luis's face and said, "Make me!"

Luis reached out and grabbed the sketch pad from under Shack's arm, surprising them both. Rian was still surprised that Luis was even trying to help.

The moment was short lived, as Shack threw out his right hand and grabbed the book back. Using his left hand, he shoved Luis to the ground. The dual actions succeeded in returning the book to Shack's grasp and sending Luis to a sitting position on the asphalt below.

"Don't make me hurt you," Shack said standing over Luis.

Luis tried to pull himself up, but Shack put his enormous hands on Luis's shoulders and pushed him back down.

"Aight. I guess you want a piece of me next?" Sandra stepped toward Shack in an aggressive manner.

"You?" Shack laughed. "I don't hit girls, especially not crippled ones."

"Crippled? I'm about to cripple you," Sandra said as she threw a left handed haymaker that missed the mark completely.

Shack laughed hysterically. He couldn't believe these kids thought they could take him.

"I mean it, don't think I won't beat up any of you. You're all crippled, basically. It's not worth my time," Shack hovered over Luis like a storm cloud as he spoke.

He didn't see Rian get to her feet. With his back to her, she pushed him from behind and sent him falling forward. He scraped his hands trying to brace himself from landing face first on the blacktop. The sketch pad fell out from under his arm as he collected his balance and whipped around.

"I said I don't hit girls, but I can make an exception." Shack stepped toward Rian with his fists up. Luis jumped between the two of them, stopping Shack's approach.

Shack picked up the sketch pad and looked over to the recess aides. All three of them were standing together, talking to one another. They paid no attention to anything else going on in the recess yard.

Glaring at Luis, Shack pointed to his left. He was signaling for Luis to meet him at the far end of the recess yard. The curvature of the exterior brick wall extended past the eye line of the recess aides. It allowed for a little privacy.

Luis understood the gesture, and he started off to the spot. Rian and Sandra chased behind Luis. Tapping her index fingers to the tips of her thumbs, Rian asked, *What are you doing?*

Excitedly Sandra declared, "He's gonna kick Shack's…."

168

Rian jumped in front of Luis and signed, *Stop!-You-don't need to-fight-him!*

Luis kept walking undeterred. His mind was made up. Shack had been asking for a fight all year. It was time someone did something about it.

As he passed by her, Rian yelled out, "Don't do this!"

Luis found Shack waiting around the bend of the round brick wall. There wasn't enough room for a game of wall ball back there, but there was more than enough room for a fight. Luis took off his jacket and tossed it onto the ground. Shack took his jacket off too, placed it on the ground and slipped the sketch pad inside of his jacket.

Rian took notice of where Shack placed her sketch pad. She considered trying to grab it back when he wasn't looking. The jacket was just in front of the wall, and Shack was between Rian and the jacket. Getting the sketch pad would be tricky for sure.

At first Luis and Shack just stood and stared at one another. Before long they were circling each other, sizing one another up. This went on for a few minutes.

"Come on, dummy. Come at me," Shack yelled at Luis.

It was Luis who swung first. He launched his right fist in Shack's direction but failed to connect. In mid-motion, Shack grabbed Luis's arm and pulled it forward, using his momentum against him. Luis tumbled to the ground.

Luis got up quickly and charged once again at Shack, lowering his head, dropping his shoulder, and going for the body. He connected this time and pushed Shack back a few feet. Shack pounded his fists down on Luis's back and ribs, and Luis punched upward into Shack's bulging stomach and chest.

From where he stood at first base, Reg Mosely got a look at the action between Shack and Luis. He ended the kickball game immediately by calling out that magic word that demanded every student's full attention.

"Fight!" he yelled, pointing in Shack and Luis's direction.

169

Every kid playing kickball ran to the hidden corner of the yard. Soon, other kids noticed the fight and headed over too. Before long, there was a large crowd watching Luis and Shack go at it.

"Fight… Fight… Fight… fight!" the kids chanted.

Luis and Shack were once again circling each other, waiting for the other to strike. Luis was having a hard time breathing from the pounding Shack delivered to his back, and Shack was bleeding, just a bit on his lower lip where Luis had landed one of his uppercuts.

"You scared? Come on, dummy. You can't hear or hit." Shack called out for the benefit of the crowd.

This time, Shack lunged toward Luis, ready to connect a devastating blow to his chin. Luis however shifted to the side and threw out his leg, tripping Shack and sending him barreling to the ground.

The students roared in celebration and called out Luis's name. He was doing something they had all imagined themselves doing at one time or another. Every one of them wanted their own shot at Shack, but they were all too afraid to take it. Luis was fighting for all of them.

"Luis! Luis! Luis!" the crowd now cheered.

Luis didn't hear the kids chanting his name, but he could sense the cheers coming from all directions. He recognized his name on their lips. He turned to look around at them all and appreciate the moment.

As Shack lay on the ground, Rian's eyes turned to his jacket. This was her chance to rescue the book without him noticing. She took a step toward it and stopped. She froze. She couldn't bring herself to even walk over to his jacket, let alone open it and retrieve her sketch pad.

What's the matter with me, she thought to herself. *Why am I such a coward?*

Shack was enraged by the kids chanting Luis's name. Luis had his back to Shack as he reveled in the moment and hyped the crowd, raising his arms like a conductor insisting his orchestra increase the intensity of the sound.

Shack got to his feet and swung clumsily at Luis, hitting him in the shoulder. Luis fell forward, but the adrenaline had taken over, and he felt nothing. He turned back and swung his right fist, landing an uppercut with a dull thud against Shack's jaw, sending his head whipping around to the right.

Shack turned and ran toward Luis. He wrapped his long arms around him and drove him to the ground. Shack was now on top of him. When he tried to punch down, Luis grabbed Shack's wrists and refused to let go. Shack thrashed, and Luis twisted himself away and got to his feet.

Shack stood up too, but the moment he got to his feet, Luis landed another punch, this time to Shack's temple, sending him back to the ground. Shack held his head as the students cheered. Luis turned and threw his arms into the air in celebration. He looked back at Shack and assumed the fight was over. Shack stayed down. People patted Luis on the back and congratulated him. He had beaten up the class bully. He stood up to and defeated Shack. It felt great!

Unfortunately for Luis, Shack wasn't finished, just yet.

Luis didn't hear Rian yell, "Look out!"

Shack came up from behind and slung his jacket over Luis's head. It was large enough to subdue Luis's arms as well. Shack drove Luis to the ground. He landed face first, unable to brace himself.

Shack rained punches down on Luis. His fists hit Luis in the back of the skull over and over. Now, the kids in the crowd yelled for Shack to stop. The noise was enough to finally capture the attention of the recess aides on the other end of the yard.

Concerned for Luis, Rian jumped on Shack's back and put her arms around his neck, as he knelt on the ground over Luis. Without much effort, Shack reached back and pulled Rian to the ground. He cocked back as if to hit her but stopped himself. He had been in a lot of fights in his life, but he had never hit a girl, and he didn't want to start today.

In his moment of hesitation, Sandra kicked her foot out and landed it squarely in Shack's chest, knocking the wind out of him. He stood up and clutched his chest, gasping for air. It was the final blow of the fight and the only part the recess aides saw.

24

dEAF NOT DEAF

"So, who threw the first punch?" Miss Hughes asked.

Rian's eyes darted across the room to Luis who was studying her face. She wasn't going to snitch, he knew that.

Luis shrugged, and Rian insisted she couldn't really remember.

They were in Miss Hughes's classroom. She was asked by Mr. Tasker to get their side of the story while he took responsibility for interrogating Shack and Sandra, two of his regulars.

"I find that hard to believe," Miss Hughes said, volleying her disappointed look from one to the other.

Shack-started it. He was bothering-Rian. I was-trying-to help, Luis signed as Mr. Rose voiced for him.

"I don't need your help," Rian said, not looking at anyone in particular. She wasn't signing for herself, and Mr. Rose wasn't translating.

"You should sign for yourself, Rian," Mr. Rose insisted.

"I'm not talking to him. Or signing. Not until he apologizes to me," she looked at Luis this time as she spoke.

Tell me-what-she said, Luis urged Mr. Rose.

"This is important. I've seen how much you've learned. You can do this. Tell Luis how you feel," Mr. Rose said encouragingly.

172

"I can't," declared Rian.

"At least try. I will help you," Mr. Rose insisted.

Reluctantly, Rian turned to Luis and clumsily signed, *I-don't need-help. I'm-not-talking-to you-until-you-apologize.*

Whatever, Luis signed slapping his hands obnoxiously.

"I don't understand. I thought you were in a fight with Gerry Shack. It's you two fighting each other again? I'm very disappointed in both of you right now," Miss Hughes signed touching her chin and dropping her eyes.

Same, Rian signed without speaking.

"Were you fighting each other?" asked Miss Hughes.

No! Rian and Luis signed in unison.

"Then what is the problem?"

Feeling worn down, Rian replied, "Luis acts like a….. Mr. Rose, what's the sign for jerk?"

"Perhaps you should find another word to use, Rian," he replied.

"He is mean to me," said Rian.

Luis tried to jump in, but Miss Hughes held up one hand and asked for patience.

"Let Rian finish," she said to him. "You'll get a chance to tell your side."

Turning to Rian she said, "Let's not make it personal. Just tell me what happened to make you feel this way."

"I thought we were friends. I can't do this," Rian confessed. "I'm not a good enough signer to tell him how I feel. Please sign for me Mr. Rose."

"You're doing great, Rian," said Mr. Rose. "Stick with it."

She was emotionally charged up and getting the words out was hard enough. Now she had to consider the signs as well.

Her hands trembled as she spoke, and her sign was disjointed and awkward at times, but Luis understood the message.

Luis-is mean, she signed. *He-doesn't like-me-because-of my-cochlear implants*.

Not-true, Luis shot back.

"Yes it is. He's mean to me because I have implants. He says I'm not really deaf," Rian said, forgetting to sign. Mr. Rose signing for her.

He says-I'm-not-really-deaf, Rian signed.

"Do you consider yourself deaf?" Miss Hughes asked.

"I know I'm not capital *D* deaf, but I am deaf," to emphasize her point, she pulled off her implant silencing the room.

Deaf, she signed, turning to Luis, pointing to her ear and then her mouth.

Luis signed big and fast making it hard for Rian to understand.

Mr. Rose spoke for Luis, "We are friends. It's true, you aren't like my other friends. They don't trust people like you."

"Francisco doesn't even know me," Rian said as she signed.

Luis responded, and Mr. Rose continued to voice for him.

"Deaf people don't trust the hearing world. Hearing people want to feel bad for us or they think we want to be like them. No way. I love being Deaf. They say we're disabled. They take pity. We don't need anyone's pity."

"That's not how I feel. I thought we were friends. I thought you knew at least that much about me." Rian spoke, her hands desperate to relay the message accurately.

We are-friends. You-are different-from-the others-who-have cochlear implants. Luis signed.

174

Furiously, Rian pressed her index and middle fingers into the back of her skull, shook her head and signed, *Not-cochlear implant! C-I! She* made sure to punctuate both letters in dramatic fashion.

"Please sign for me," she said, turning to Mr. Rose. "I want to get this right."

Mr. Rose nodded to her.

"I'm not different from other kids with cochlear implants. I'm not different from hearing kids. I'm a person first, just like you, or Hassan or Elisha. Do you know other people with cochlear implants? Do you know how lonely it feels to be trapped between the hearing world and the Deaf world? They think I'm Deaf, you say I'm not. Why does it matter?

She put her bent fingers behind her ear.

"I know what this means. It's an insult. I don't want you to use that sign anymore.

Luis felt a wave of guilt wash over him. He didn't mean to use the sign, but it was an old habit. After a moment, his hands raced furiously as he explained.

"Deafness is my culture," Mr. Rose voiced. "Wayne is Black. Hassan is Muslim. You are Irish. You're not Deaf the same way I'm not Irish. You could have been Deaf, like me, but instead you have an implant."

"That wasn't my choice! I know I'm different. I know I'm not a member of Deaf culture, but so what? Is that a requirement to be a friend? Should that allow you to treat me like an outsider?

I am an outsider too, you know. I can hear with these things, but people still think I'm deaf and treat me like I'm deaf. They don't want to partner with me, they don't want to sit with me. At least not at this school. The only people who think I'm hearing are you, Hassan, and Wayne. At least you have a group. You have a culture. All I had was you guys, and now I don't even have that."

Turning to Luis, Miss Hughes said, "Luis, you don't judge Hassan because he's Muslim, do you?"

175

No. signed Luis.

"Or Wayne, because he's Black?"

No, Luis repeated.

"Rian's mother made a choice early in her life. She chose to give Rian the chance to be a part of the hearing world, because that's where she lives. Just like your mother would have never considered implants for you, because the Deaf world is where she lives. Having friends and appreciating their differences is what makes life great."

Turning to Rian, Mr. Rose said, "Most people born deaf are not born into Deaf families. When a Deaf person sees someone with an implant they see it as a lost opportunity for someone to be a part of their community. ASL is the key to their culture. When parents choose a hearing world for their child, it means one less member of the Deaf community.

Deaf people, like Luis, are watching their small world become even smaller," Mr. Rose concluded.

"That's why it's so important that you're learning ASL. That is how you get access to the Deaf community. Most Deaf people are welcoming people. Just like you, Luis." Miss Hughes said, resting her eyes on Luis.

The phone rang. Miss Hughes got up to answer and after a few "Okays," she hung it up.

"Rian, you mother is here. Grab your stuff," she said.

Rian cringed at the thought of having to explain all of this to her mother. Her mind quickly wandered to possible punishments. She just got over being grounded.

Philly really is turning me into a delinquent, she thought to herself.

"Before you go, do you think you and Luis are ready to forgive each other? Friendship is always worth a second chance. Don't you think?" asked Miss Hughes.

Rian and Luis looked at one another. Their expressions revealed their answer. A moment later they signed the words.

"Good," Miss Hughes said, very pleased with herself. "Now you better get moving."

Rian grabbed her bag and unzipped it, ready to put her books inside.

"My sketch pad," she called out. "He still has my sketch pad!"

"Who?" asked Miss Hughes, "Who has your sketch pad?"

"Shack!" she exclaimed. "Shack has my sketch pad!"

25

FOOTPRINTS

Rian's contribution to the fight was enough to earn her a suspension from school for the rest of the week. Joanna was so upset with Rian, she grounded her. Since none of her friends lived in the neighborhood, the only part of the punishment that bothered Rian was not being allowed to use her brand new cellphone.

On the last day of her suspension from school, Joanna returned the phone to Rian. That morning, they made a trip to the audiologist, Rian's hearing doctor. Her new cochlear implant was finally ready to be picked up! The visit was a good distraction for them both. Rian had been giving Joanna the cold shoulder all week, but now she was too excited to keep it up.

The new implant had a lot of cool new features. The audiologist explained that it was Bluetooth enabled. That meant that she could connect it to her cellphone and hear the audio go directly to her implant. Once she saw the excitement on her daughter's face, Joanna no longer had the heart to keep the cellphone from her. On their way home, Rian watched YouTube videos and streamed her favorite music, thanks to the magic of Bluetooth.

Later, after they finished dinner, Rian ran to her room and shut her door for the night. She had done the same exact thing every night that week. She pretended like she was upset with Joanna and with being grounded. She told her mother that she had a book to read, and she didn't want to be bothered.

In truth, Rian wasn't mad at Joanna for grounding her. The routine of locking herself in the room every night was part of a larger plan. Rian had been biding her time, waiting for an opportunity to get her sketch pad back. Tonight was her night to act!

Rian had no intention of reading her book that evening. As always, she locked her door, but instead of jumping back into her novel, she opened up her bedroom window and crawled out onto the patio roof. Careful not to make a lot of noise, she shimmied down the front porch post and ran down the steps, heading for Holmesburg Circle.

Rian crawled through the opening in the green chain link fence. The ground was still saturated from heavy rain that had fallen the night before. She struggled to get herself through, and when she came out the other side her pants, shoes, hands, and face were covered in mud.

What am I doing? I'm already in trouble. If I get caught…

She shook off her concern and focused on the task at hand. She knew there was no turning back. She was going to that house, and she was going to get her sketch pad back.

She pulled herself to her feet and headed for Shack's abandoned house. The sun had almost set, so as she approached the back, she saw the structure, or what was left of it, in greater detail.

The place was old and long forgotten. Short and narrow, the stone-encrusted face featured varied shades of stacked slate with large gaping wounds where mortar had given way over time. Exposed sheets of white plaster flanked what was left of the stone facade.

Almost all of the window glass was gone, as trees and shrubs attempted to reclaim the house's earthy foundation. The plywood sheet meant to conceal the inside of the house lay flat on the ground. She could see it was covered in graffiti. Carefully, Rian walked inside.

The house felt empty. Standing alone, Rian suddenly understood the draw of a place like this. She could do whatever she wanted here and there was no one to stop her. The thought made her feel empowered.

She saw the piece of mortar she had tossed through the window Halloween night lying beside a shattered coffee mug. The cigarette lighter sat next to the mug. She picked up the lighter and placed it in her pocket. Then she grabbed the mortar and heaved it with all her might. It pierced a piece of wallpaper. Instead of smashing into pieces, it disappeared into the wall.

She got up to inspect the brittle, water-stained wallpaper. She grabbed the punctured sheet and peeled it back. The wallpaper concealed a giant hole in the plaster. The hole went straight through to the adjoining living room. Rian peered through the hole and saw an old couch against the opposite wall. Nestled in the center of the dank, grey, musty sofa was the piece of mortar.

Rian turned her attention to the oven. She wasn't here to play, she had a purpose. She wanted her sketch pad. She had no idea what condition it might be in, but it was hers, and she wanted it back.

Rian opened the oven and found it, exactly where she thought she would. Sitting atop a pile of other people's stuff. She pulled it out.

Flipping through the pages, she saw that Shack had destroyed just about every drawing in the book. There was no effort to reframe the drawings as idiotic, the way he had done to the picture of her father. Now, he had just taken a blue pen and run it over the pages. A moment's worth of scribble, designed to undue hours and hours of her hard work.

She felt surprised looking at the drawings. Not because he had defaced them, she expected that. She was surprised that seeing her hard work destroyed did not make her cry. She fully expected to bawl her eyes out over the book. In place of her sadness was anger. She was furious about what he had done to her drawings. She needed to do something but had no idea what she could possibly do to get him back.

The first picture in the book, a picture of her dog Petey, remained untouched. It was the very first picture she drew in that sketch pad, and in a way, it was her favorite. It wasn't her best work, and it would never win any awards, but it was important to her.

When her mother gave her the sketch pad years ago, Rian carried it around for a week, trying to decide what to draw first. The book was so beautiful with its leather cover and spiral binding that she wanted every picture to be a masterpiece. When she finally decided to sketch something, Petey was her muse.

She chose Petey because of how much she loved him. When her mom and dad fought, Petey was always there for her. She was not going to abandon that picture. Not in this place.

Rian slung her backpack off of her shoulder, unzipped the top and slipped the sketchpad inside. After a moment's consideration, she took the other items from the oven and placed them on the counter.

Hidden in the back of the oven was Mrs. Bae-Huley's book. She pulled it out and looked it over. She was about to close the oven door when something caught her eye. She glanced down to inspect what it was.

Looking inside the oven, she saw something shimmering in the very back corner. It was easy to miss, as it was covered in years of baked-on food grime, dust, and dirt. Carefully, she reached in and pulled out an old pair of glasses.

They were thick, angular framed, gold-rimmed glasses. The thin frame was slightly bent.

He stole someone's glasses, Rian thought to herself. *What a creep.*

Suddenly, an idea came to her. A plan. A wicked, cunning, risky, vengeful plan. A way she and the others could make Shack pay for all the misery he'd caused them and the other sixth graders at John Hancock Elementary.

She placed Mrs. Bae-Huley's book into her bag, and then, one-by-one, she placed the other items back into the oven, including the sketch pad. When she came to the glasses, she decided to hold onto them.

These could be useful, she thought to herself.

Not wanting to break the glasses, she placed them gingerly into her pocket and closed the oven door.

From where she stood, she could see footprints all over the floor. She looked at her muddy shoes. These were her footprints. The rain the night before made the trail a mess and she tracked the mess right into the kitchen.

I better clean this up or he'll know someone was here, she thought to herself. She looked around for something she could use to wipe the prints off the floor. She found an old yellow dish towel in the sink.

The sun had set, and the kitchen had scarcely any light to fill the room. She was lucky she noticed the prints at all. She got down on her knees for a closer look.

She needed the lighter to inspect the mess. The footprint belonged to a size 6 shoe. Her size. There were a series of concentric circles on the top and bottom of the print that looked like a bullseye, with wavy lines running horizontally from the top of the shoe to the bottom.

Rian turned her ankle, inspected her shoe and confirmed the print was hers. She thought about how dangerous it would be to not have noticed. Shack would surely recognize the prints when he came back to the house. He might even be smart enough to track them.

She knelt down to wipe up the mud. Crawling around on all fours she managed to erase the evidence. From where she crouched she could see the Ouija board directly in front of her. There was red wax from one of the candles splattered across the board. She grabbed it, wiped the sole of her shoe with the rag and sat back down at the kitchen table.

The board gave Rian an idea. She reached into her pocket and pulled out the cigarette lighter. Carefully, she leaned over and grabbed the red candle from off the floor and ignited the wick. She sat for a few moments, watching the flame dance. When a pool of wax approximately one fingernail deep surrounded the wick, Rian dipped her finger in the hot liquid.

She watched as it hardened around the tip of her finger, creating a wax cast the size of a thumbnail. Dipping her finger in once again, Rian smeared the congealing red wax around the letter *T* on the Ouija board. Another plunge into the wax allowed her to circle the letter *I*, then *M*. She darkened the circles by encasing them in layer after layer of red wax, until it was unmistakable. The name *TIM* was circled on the Ouija board.

She got up and rested the board in the center of the table for Shack to find, wiped her hand with the yellow rag and collected the books and the glasses.

Bang. There was a loud thump that came from a room directly above the kitchen, startling Rian, and causing her to drop her backpack.

What was that?

She moved toward the door and turned back to give the house one last look. She saw the yellow rag sitting on the kitchen table. She hurried back to the table and grabbed it, shoving it into her front pocket. As she headed out the door she saw more footprints.

Don't be dumb, she thought to herself pulling the rag out of her pocket and getting back down again to wipe up the mess.

The prints were fresh and thick with mud. The saturated rag was useless. Rian just smeared the print across the floor.

Come on, I want to get out of here. You have to be careful, Rian. You can't leave evidence.

She pulled her shirt cuff over her hand and used it to remove the mud slick from the floor. Before she could pull herself up she saw two more prints. She thought they led out of the kitchen. After a closer look she saw they actually led into the kitchen from the dark hallway in front of her. The same hallway where she thought she saw someone watching her Halloween night.

Even more bizarre, the print on the floor was not her shoe print. This one had a series of diamond shapes that ran the length of the shoe, from toe to heel. It was clearly made by a much larger shoe.

BANG!

A loud thud, like something falling over, crashed above her, in a room on the second floor of the house.

Shack! Rian's mind screamed out.

Rian jumped to her feet and ran out the door as fast as she could, never once looking back.

26

THE PLAN

Rian unzipped her backpack and showed them the book. Mrs. Bae-Huley's *Highways* teacher's edition.

You are-crazy! Hassan blurted out spinning his finger by his temple.

She pushed the book back into her bag and zipped it up, looking suspiciously at the other students in the lunchroom.

She told them that she got the idea after going back to the house. She found a pair of glasses that looked like the ones Mr. Herman described in his story. She didn't mention that she felt she wasn't alone in the house. The logical part of her brain told her it was Shack and that she almost got caught.

That night however, she kept thinking about that shadowy figure at the end of the hallway and the muddy footprints on the floor. She knew it made no sense, but she felt like the other person in the house with her was not a person at all. She felt like it was something supernatural.

Although she told herself the thought was ridiculous, she was certain there was something there. Something she could use, that they all could use, to exact revenge on Shack. She had Mrs. Bae-Huley's book and a plan to make Shack pay.

The plan was risky but simple. They were going to convince Shack that he was being haunted. Haunted by the ghost of Timothy Rollins.

"He did not believes Halloween night. Why he believes now?" Hassan grilled Rian on the particulars of the plan.

"He doesn't know that we know about that night. We can leave a bunch of clues that will make him think it's a ghost," Rian answered.

"I like it," said Sandra. "We can scare him, and then we can jump him!"

"That's not what I had in mind," Rian replied.

What do we do? Luis asked.

Rian explained they would have to get Mrs. Bae-Huley's book into the classroom and onto her desk. She slipped the book out of her bag once again. Keeping it close to her body, she opened the book and showed them her handiwork. The letters *TR* were scribbled all over the pages with a red marker.

"When she opens it, she'll see the letters written in red marker and freak out," Rian explained.

"You trashed Bae-Huley's book? That's beautiful!" Sandra gushed.

I don't-understand, signed Luis.

"She will show the book to the class and want to know who is responsible. Shack knows he had the book. When he sees *TR* written on the pages he'll think it's Timothy Rollins," Rian explained.

Are you-sure? Luis asked skeptically.

Wayne interrupted, "Shack's dumb. He won't get it."

"He will. Who else could TR be? Besides, when he goes back to the house to check, he'll find a message I left for him there too. He will be scared out of his mind."

"And then we jump him!" Sandra yelled.

"How you know he will be scared?" asked Hassan.

"That place is creepy. When I was there the other day, I was creeped out. I thought I was being haunted. It's sure to work."

Rian placed her right fist into the opposite palm and raised her hands together.

Help-me? Rian asked her friends.

Here we go, she thought to herself. Rian finished her sandwich and watched Ms. Martinez walk to the other side of the lunchroom. She raised her hand to get Ms. Martinez's attention.

Ms. Martinez was a grandparent who volunteered for lunch duty. She wore red-rimmed glasses with large round lenses that perpetually seemed as though they were going to fall off the end of her nose. She slowly made her way over to Rian.

"Can I go to the bathroom?" she asked Ms. Martinez.

"Don't be long," Ms. Martinez growled in a deep throaty voice. "It's almost time for recess."

She turned away, and Rian stood up. Luis grabbed her by the arm and pulled her back down.

"What are you doing?" she asked.

Not-by yourself! Luis signed to her.

"Hassan's right," said Sandra. "You need someone to get your back. In case Bae-Huley shows up."

"OK. Hassan, you come with me," Rian suggested.

"Me?" Hassan blurted out, pointing to himself. "No way happening!"

"No, you need me," said Sandra. "They're not gonna hear Bae-Huley coming."

187

"You're still on recess detention. Mr. Tasker will notice if you're missing. It's too risky," said Rian. She pointed to her ear and said, "Hassan can hear if someone is coming. We'll use his FM."

Hassan reached into his pocket and pulled out the pen-shaped microphone.

"This is bad idea," he said, but it was clear Rian's mind was made up. She waited for Hassan to bring Ms. Martinez back to the table.

"Martin, can I go too?" Hassan asked.

"It's Martinez. Mar. Teen. Ez," Mrs. Martinez pointed at a mouthful of pearly white dentures as she over-pronounced each syllable in her name. "Now, let me hear you."

"Mar-tin-ez," Hassan said. It was hard enough for Hassan to pronounce her name, but in the cafeteria, he could barely hear her.

"Mar. Teeeeen-Ez," she said again. "If you want me to let you go, you have to ask properly."

Hassan ran his hands through his floppy black hair and thought for a moment. He held out his FM microphone.

"What's that?" she asked.

"Say again," Hassan asked.

"What is that?" Ms. Martinez repeated. "Am I supposed to speak into it?" She leaned in close to the microphone and yelled each syllable.

"Mar. Teen. Ez," she bellowed.

"Mar-een-ez," Hassan repeated.

With a roll of her eyes, Mrs. Martinez shooed her hand in the direction of the cafeteria entrance and said, "Close enough, I suppose."

She turned to Rian and asked, "What are you waiting for?"

They left the cafeteria together, passed the bathrooms, and turned the corner toward Mrs. Bae-Huley's classroom. There wasn't a teacher in the building that would stop them in the hallway, and they knew it. The teachers considered lunch sacred. Unless they were followed by smoke, Hancock teachers had no interest in finding out why students were in the hall during their lunch break.

They reached Mrs. Bae-Huley's room and were surprised to find her sitting at her desk, scooping out the last bit of orange Jell-O from a plastic cup. This wasn't part of the plan. Normally the sixth-grade teachers ate in the staff lounge. A mysterious room in the school where no students were ever permitted.

"What are we going to do?" Rian whispered just outside of the door.

"Huh?" Hassan asked, unable to hear Rian's whisper-level voice.

Unaware of his own volume, Rian put her finger to her lips. Her wide eyes did the shushing.

Hassan whispered back, "What do we do?"

"We need a distraction," Rian whispered again.

From where they stood, they could see Mr. Herman's room. It was empty. The clock on the far wall read 12:20. They had fifteen minutes to plant the book before the end of recess.

Sitting on Mr. Herman's desk was Rian's FM microphone. It gave her an idea.

She darted into Mr. Herman's room and snatched the microphone off his desk. She placed it by an old radio resting on the long air vent beneath the window. She waved her hand urging Hassan to come join her in the room.

"Give me your FM," she said to him.

Hassan handed it over, and she put it around her neck.

Then, she turned on the radio filling the room with classic hits from the 1970s. A man's high-pitched voice proclaimed his intention to stay alive. She turned the volume down.

"When I give you the signal, put the microphone next to the speaker and turn the music up. Then hide under Mr. Herman's desk so no one sees you." She handed him her clunky silver microphone.

"I think this will not work," said Hassan.

"It will work. Just don't mess it up," Rian tried to assure him. "Ready?"

"No," Hassan answered.

Rian walked out of the room. She moved into the empty classroom across from Mrs. Bae-Huley's. Peering around the corner, she watched Mrs. Bae-Huley pour the last little bit of her diet Coke down her throat.

She held Hassan's microphone close to her mouth and said, "Now. Hassan, do it now."

The silence that followed convinced Rian that Hassan didn't hear her. Before she could repeat the command, loud music blared out of the room and was sent directly to the FM speaker in Mrs. Bae-Huley's classroom.

The sudden burst of music out of Rian's speaker, on the other side of the classroom, caused Mrs. Bae-Huley to jump out of her seat and knock over her empty can of soda. It rattled around the floor as she turned her head left then right, trying to determine where the noise was coming from. It was not immediately clear that it was coming from Rian's speaker.

Once she located the source of the music, she ran to the speaker and turned it off. The music, however, continued playing from another room. Determined to shut it down, she followed the sound toward Mr. Herman's classroom.

"Hide, Hassan, hide. She's coming," the urgency in Rian's voice was clear, even though she kept her volume low.

I hope he heard me, she thought to herself.

She watched Mrs. Bae-Huley walk into Mr. Herman's room, then she immediately shot across the hall.

Shack's desk was in the front. Although she preferred to keep him as far from her as possible, Mrs. Bae-Huley practiced the time-honored tradition of keeping troublemakers close to tamp down their antics. A convenient situation for Rian since it would allow Shack to see the book on Mrs. Bae-Huley's desk right away.

Many of the desks in the room, including Shack's, were covered with papers and books. Reaching into her backpack, Rian pulled out Mrs. Bae-Huley's big book and placed it in the center of her desk.

Quickly, she ran to the door but stopped before exiting. Out of the corner of her eye she saw a red, dry erase marker on Jamilah Masullah's desk. She grabbed the marker and turned back to Shack's desk.

Looking up at the clock she knew she was just about out of time, but she had one more detail she wanted to add. Among the papers scattered around Shack's desk was a long-forgotten vocabulary packet. Rian took the cap off Jamilah's red marker and scribbled two large letters over the first page. Not satisfied, she turned to the next page and the next until every page had the letters *TR* written on it.

This last-minute detail cost Rian precious seconds. She heard Mrs. Bae-Huley's wooden heels galloping toward the room. Without a moment to think, she ducked behind Mrs. Bae-Huley's desk.

It was not a good place to hide. Mrs. Bae-Huley would surely see her when she sat down, but there was nowhere else to go. Holding her breath, Rian closed her eyes and waited to be caught. She imagined getting blamed for stealing and destroying the book. She would be suspended for sneaking around the room during lunch. Worst of all, Shack would know that she was TR.

Then, just as the cliché states, she was saved by the bell. Recess was over. Mrs. Bae-Huley turned away from her desk and walked back out the door. When she was gone, Rian resurfaced and ran to Mr. Herman's room.

"Hassan? Hassan?" she called out.

Hassan poked his head out from the coat closet.

"We need to go. Now!" she said, exasperated.

Rian and Hassan slipped out of the building and into the recess yard. The cold November air was an instant reminder that she left her coat in the cafeteria. It was an oversight, but given the number of jackets, gloves, hats, and shoes in the lost and found, her coat was not likely to raise a red flag.

In fact, no one seemed to notice the two of them as they came out of the building. They eased themselves into line with the rest of their class as if they had never been gone.

It was business as usual on the way back to the room. Mrs. Bae-Huley expected quiet. She made it a point to say, "Hands on hips, fingers on lips" anytime they walked through the hallway. It was a childish thing to say to a group of sixth graders and was no doubt a remnant of her days as a kindergarten teacher.

By the time they lined up outside the classroom, Mr. Rose was already sitting in his chair in the front of the class, hands folded over his crossed legs.

"Girls," Mrs. Bae-Huley spoke as though she were choosing the victor in a battle of Roman gladiators.

The ladies flowed single file into the classroom. With no coat to hang up, Rian went directly to her seat.

"Boys," Mrs. Bae-Huley announced.

Mrs. Bae-Huley was halfway to her desk when she saw it. The glossy red cover and bone-white spiral binding encasing the massive book. Her pace quickened. Upon reaching her desk, Mrs. Bae-Huley swept the book into her arms and nestled it in her bosom, allowing a squeal of ecstasy to barely escape her lips drawn back in a long, tight, toothy grin.

Rian, Luis, Hassan, Sandra and Wayne all noticed her exuberance, but no one else paid any attention, including Shack.

Lovingly, Mrs. Bae-Huley rested the book on her desk. She caressed the cover with her open palm as if she were petting a cocker spaniel. She grabbed the phone off the wall and dialed extension 4124.

"Cindy, it's Cil. I got it. The book. I have no idea. There's no note. Someone left it on my desk when I went to pick up the kids." As she spoke, she opened the cover and flipped pages.

Her expression morphed from exaltation to horror. The red letters *TR* were scrawled across page after page of her beloved manual. She flipped the pages one after another, seeing those letters again and again. *TR. TR.*

"Cindy, I have to go," Mrs. Bae-Huley hung up the phone without further explanation and turned her attention to the class.

She slammed the book closed, clasped it in both hands and held it out in front of her body like a talisman used to ward off a demon.

"Do any of you know how this book got on my desk?" The anger in her voice was palpable.

Everyone stopped what they were doing and turned to look. Shack immediately recognized the book. His eyes grew wide, and his body stiffened. He scanned the room. Rian turned away before he cast his glance in her direction.

"I need everyone to take their seats." The seriousness in Mrs. Bae-Huley's tone was matched only by the haste with which the students obeyed her order.

"Someone took this book from me. It's been missing for months. It miraculously appeared on my desk with the letters *TR* written all over it."

She stopped speaking and looked at each student one at a time. You could see the gears at work as she thought of each student's first and last names, looking for someone with the initials *TR*. A detail that hadn't occurred to Rian until this instant. Fortunately, no one in the class shared those initials.

Shack shifted in his seat uncomfortably, trying not to bring any undue attention on himself. He dropped his gaze from the book to his desk. He saw the packet and the letters *TR* written across the front.

Mrs. Bae-Huley stood in the center of the room pacing back and forth, clasping the book in both hands. Shack grabbed the packet and flipped it over. He was shocked to see the letters *TR* written on both sides.

He yanked it off his desk, drawing the attention of Mrs. Bae-Huley. He thrust the packet below the desk and kept his hands over it as it lay on his lap.

"Gerard," Mrs. Bae-Huley's accusing tone now focused on Shack. "Do you know anything about this?"

"No," said Shack with a nervous quiver in his voice that did not go unnoticed.

"What were you doing during recess today?" Mrs. Bae-Huley's question suggested the interrogation had begun.

"I was with Ben the whole time," Shack said, turning to Ben to confirm his alibi.

Mrs. Bae-Huley turned her attention to Ben. "Is that true?"

"Yeah," said Ben, not expressing any concern whatsoever about the situation. "We were playing with Lucas."

Mrs. Bae-Huley now turned the burning embers in her pupils on Lucas. He didn't speak, but he nodded his head in agreement, further infuriating Mrs. Bae-Huley.

"Well, someone is responsible for this. Someone in this room thinks it is funny to deface personal property. I want you all to understand that when I find out who did this, everyone involved is going to be in a world of hurt. So, if you know something, now is the time to talk. If I have to find out on my own, the lord himself won't be able to save you."

She spoke in a low, threatening tone, making eye contact with anyone not looking down at their desk.

The silence was unbearable. Three minutes passed as Mrs. Bae-Huley waited for someone to speak. Someone to say something. Those three minutes felt like hours to Rian.

What was she doing? She had never done anything like this before. Living in Philadelphia was turning her into a criminal. Sure, Shack was a creep, but her mother always told her two wrongs don't make a right. She was sure what she had done was wrong, and worse than that, she was certain she was going to get caught.

She imagined Mrs. Bae-Huley's investigation. First, she would find out Ms. Martinez allowed Hassan and her to go to the bathroom right around the time of the incident. She would further learn that they never came back. The evidence of their crime was her abandoned coat, still sitting in the cafeteria. There were so many loose ends.

Mercifully, those wretched three minutes came to an end. Taking a deep breath and a long exhale, Mrs. Bae-Huley strode over to her desk, placed the book down gingerly, and spoke softly.

"Open up your Writer's Journal," she said with an unsettling calm in her voice.

Rian looked back at Shack. With the packet still on his lap, he tore off a page, folded it three ways and crushed it into his back pocket. For the rest of the afternoon no one in Mrs. Bae-Huley's room made a peep. Not one sound.

27

GIVE IT BACK

The next day, Mrs. Bae-Huley's class was back at it, working in the computer lab. They had spent over a month straight working in the lab. From the moment she lost her beloved teacher's edition, she was unable to fill a forty five minute block of time normally spent reading historical fiction, poetry and personal narratives. For the first two weeks she had new assignments for the class to complete every day, but she had given up on that weeks earlier. Now, they were working on a long term project with no end in sight: biographical presentations of famous world leaders.

They had an inordinate amount of time to work on the assignment. Some kids enjoyed the down time, choosing to play games or watch videos instead of working, but Rian had grown tired of it. They hadn't touched their textbook in ages. She kind of missed it.

Shack spent almost the entire month in the lab watching YouTube videos and playing video games. To Rian's delight and everyone else's dismay, Mrs. Bae-Huley announced at the beginning of the class that today would be the last day to finish their presentations. Shack no choice but to work on his.

He hacked away at his keyboard on a slide about Margaret Thatcher, or as he called her, the "Iron Lung." He had a really difficult time trying to figure out why that was her nickname.

His fingers jabbed one key after the next, bludgeoning letters onto the screen. He was putting the finishing touches on slide number two of his presentation. The slide described Margaret Thatcher as a woman "as strong as a man." It featured a picture of Queen Elizabeth.

He added a new slide but stopped when suddenly his cursor moved to the taskbar at the top of the screen by itself.

Shack stared at the screen bewildered. He looked left, then right, then back at the screen. The cursor hung over an icon on the taskbar that changed the color of the text.

Amazingly, all by itself, the cursor clicked on the icon. A palate of small colored squares appeared in a pop-up window on the screen. The cursor moved to the red square and selected the color.

Shack leaned in closer as three words appeared one letter at a time on the screen. The message, written in all caps, was simple. It read:

GIVE IT BACK.

Shack recoiled. Whatever this was, it sounded threatening. He turned around and got Ben's attention.

"Look," Shack said, tapping his hand on the computer table. "Check this out."

Hassan watched Shack from across the room. The moment Shack turned away from the screen, Hassan hit the Control key and the *Z* key simultaneously on his keyboard. The cryptic red message disappeared from Shack's screen.

Ben peered over his monitor to take a look.

"What?" he asked.

"What do you think? I didn't write that!" exclaimed Shack.

"There's nothing on your screen," Ben said.

Shack looked back at the screen and saw that the message in red was gone. Ben slouched back behind his computer.

Certain Ben wasn't paying attention, Hassan pressed the Control key again, only this time he pressed down on the V key, returning the words to the screen.

GIVE IT BACK.

Shack jumped out of his seat, sending his chair into the table behind him. "Who's doing that?" he demanded, looking around the room. The class was startled at his sudden outburst breaking the silence that had filled the lab.

"Doing what?" asked Mrs. Bae-Huley.

"Writing on my screen," he said exasperated. "Someone is writing on my screen."

Mrs. Bae-Huley got up and walked over to Shack's computer. The moment she stood up, Hassan deleted the words. When she came to his table, all Mrs. Bae-Huley saw was Shack's blank slide.

"How long is this presentation?" asked Mrs. Bae-Huley. "This looks like you've only got about two slides here."

"Three! Look," he answered back, pointing to his screen.

"It's blank," Mrs. Bae-Huley said disgustedly. "We've been here for two weeks, and this is all you've done."

"It's been a month," Shack replied stupidly.

She paged through his presentation, what little there was of it. He misspelled Thatcher twice and incorrectly identified her home as Liverpool. "Where is the rest of your work?" Mrs. Bae-Huley demanded.

"No. Wait. Someone is writing on my screen in red letters," Shack said, pointing at the screen.

"I don't see anything on this screen, Mr. Shack. I do see a red letter in your future, though. A big red F. I suggest you get back to work. These presentations are due tomorrow."

"Someone wrote…" Shack stopped, not wanting to say the words for fear of incriminating himself. "There were words in red. Words that I didn't type."

"I suggest you take the remaining time left in this period and get it together. Don't think for one minute that I am going to accept any excuses from you for not being finished. Including and especially that some aliens took over your computer. Lord, you must think I was born yesterday."

Before Mrs. Bae-Huley was back in her seat, Hassan had a new message ready to go. With one click, it appeared on Shack's screen.

GET EVERYTHING YOU STOLE AND PUT
IT IN THE KILN. TOMORROW!!!!

Putting the stuff in the kiln was Wayne's idea. The plan, as Rian understood it, was to scare Shack into returning everything. Wayne suggested they tell Shack to put the stuff in the kiln because it was where Timmy Rollins "got lit up". He said it would be epic to expose him in front of Mrs. Miller's kiln to the rest of the class. Rian and the others agreed.

Wayne however, had a secret. He planned to push Shack into the kiln and lock him inside, with the stuff. Lock him in just the way Timothy Rollins had been locked inside the kiln. He kept it a secret, because he knew the others wouldn't approve.

When they were in fifth grade, Shack and Wayne had had a fight at Byberry Park, not far from the school. Shack was surprised to see Wayne there, since he was a bus rider, and Millbrook Park wasn't his neighborhood. It didn't take long for the two boys to trash talk and eventually get into a fight.

By all accounts, Wayne got the best of Shack at first. Wayne was small and scrappy. Shack was large and slow. He couldn't manage to get his hands on Wayne. In the end, it was Shack who got the better of Wayne by pushing him backward over a rocking, spring-mounted hippopotamus. Wayne landed hard on his back, and had the wind knocked out of him.

While still on the ground, Shack kneeled on Wayne's shoulders and pinned him to the dirt. Wayne was unable to wrestle free, and Shack pummeled him mercilessly. The fight stuck with Wayne for a year as he waited for his opportunity to get revenge. Now, the opportunity was about to presented itself.

Behind his computer, Shack was starting to panic. First, the book showed up from out of nowhere and now this. Someone or something was out to get him. Someone or something knew about the house. Knew about the oven. What exactly did this person want returned? He leaned into the computer and asked, "Give back what?"

Again in red letters and in all caps, Hassan wrote the word:

EVERYTHING!

Quickly, Hassan copied the word and pasted it again and again. The message written in red letters filled Shack's screen. It repeated twenty times, then thirty times, and then forty.

EVERYTHING! EVERYTHING! EVERYTHING! EVERYTHING!

EVERYTHING! EVERYTHING! EVERYTHING! EVERYTHING!

EVERYTHING! EVERYTHING! EVERYTHING! EVERYTHING!

Now, Shack was threating the computer, speaking to it in low tones. Leaning into the machine, he whispered the words, "You're dead. I am going to find out who you are, and I am going to kill you."

Sandra, sitting two seats down from Shack, kept her eyes forward and her hand, holding Hassan's FM microphone, pointed directly at Shack.

Hassan signaled to Sandra by pointing to his ear and shaking his head. Even with the microphone pointed in his direction, he couldn't hear Shack. Sandra understand the message. She put her thumb to her chin, wiggled her index finger and signed, "Who?"

Hassan nodded, turned back to his computer and typed.

YOU KNOW WHO I AM.

The message caused a lump in Shack's throat to swell. He didn't want to ask the question, but he felt he had no choice. Looking around the room once more, in a whisper, he asked, "Who are you?"

A name appeared on his screen, one letter at a time. Not initials but words, written in large red capital letters. The screen read:

TIMOTHY ROLLINS

28

HOT WATER

While Hassan and Wayne were toying with Shack in the computer lab, Luis was hiding in a bathroom stall playing Gollum Garden on his cell phone. Checking the time, he saw the period was almost over. He got up, placed the phone in his back pocket, and exited the stall.

Standing in front of the mirror, Luis turned on the water to wash his hands. At the same moment that water shot from the faucet, Luis sensed a toilet flush behind him. He had never heard a toilet flush, but he could feel the intense rush of water from the high capacity bowls and the echo it stirred in the small-tiled bathroom all around him.

He pumped three times expecting pink hand soap to fall from a black wall dispenser, but the third push confirmed the thing was empty. A second flush rumbled behind him. He peaked in the mirror and saw three empty stalls behind him, each with their doors open.

Luis ran his hands under the faucet but pulled them out immediately. The water was scalding hot. Bending over, he buried his hands between his legs to subdue the pain. After a moment he pulled his hands to his face and saw blisters forming on his palms.

Steam rose from the sink bowl as water inched closer to the edge. He grabbed the X-shaped porcelain hot water knob to turn it off which sent a bolt of pain shooting through his hand. He tried to turn it, but it didn't move. Confused, he moved his hand to the cold water handle, but it did not move either. Water continued to gush from the spigot.

A third flush sent Luis whipping around to face the toilets. He looked at the stall directly behind him. The water was still. He checked the other two stalls and saw the water in the bowls was as placid as the community pool in September.

He felt another flush.

There must be something wrong with the plumbing, he thought.

The water in the sink was now spilling over the side of the bowl. He walked back over and tried once again to turn it off.

The rising steam condensed on the mirror in front of him as he tried with all of his might to turn either handle in either direction. Nothing gave.

The hot water coming from the sink was beading up on his face as the temperature in the bathroom increased. Luis didn't know if the droplets on his head were from steam or sweat. Water flowed over the sides of the sink and pooled on the floor around his feet. He could feel the warmth radiating through the soles of his shoes.

He reached for a brown paper towel and wiped his brow. He decided it was time to tell someone about the problem. He wiped the steam from the mirror to check his face before he left and saw a boy standing directly behind him.

Luis jumped and turned around instinctively. It wasn't uncommon for people to sneak up behind him, but the door to the bathroom was within his view, and he was certain no one had entered the room.

He was even more startled after he turned around again and saw no one in the room with him. His head snapped left and right, looking for the boy in the mirror, but there was no one.

Completely freaked out, Luis backed away from the sink in the direction of the door. He was startled to see the hot water knob turn itself off. The water stopped running. He looked at his palms and was relieved to see the blisters were gone. Even stranger, the floor was dry.

Except for the steam on the mirror, there was almost no evidence to suggest anything unusual had just happened. Luis walked back to the sink and looked at the fogged-up mirror. He wasn't crazy. The steam had to come from somewhere.

He looked around again, trying to find the water that, just moments earlier, he watched fall to the floor. He ran his finger over the white porcelain sink and found it was bone dry.

Then he found himself staring in amazement at the mirror. Letters started to appear in the steam, the way they do when someone presses their fingers to the glass. A word formed. Then a second word and finally a third. He could feel the presence of someone in the bathroom with him, pressing their finger to the glass, but he saw no one. He was frozen.

His feet were glued to the floor. The words were a message. A warning. Something sinister was happening, and he had to warn the others. Scribbled in the faded steam were the words, "Give It Back!"

29

FORECLOSURE

Julio and Jennifer could tell something wasn't right with Luis that night. On his way home, Julio picked up Arroz con Pollo from Luis's favorite restaurant, Ranchito.   To his parents' surprise he barely touched his chicken or rice and hurried upstairs to his room as soon as he was excused.

That night Luis used his cell phone to investigate Shack's abandoned house. First, he tried to find it using a satellite map by zooming in on Millbrook Park. He found Hancock easily because it was a giant brick circle just below an airport. Zooming in further, he spotted Holmesburg Circle and followed it up to the tree line at the end of the cul-de-sac. He found the house and was surprised to find it had an address.

1669 Croydon St., Philadelphia, Pennsylvania.

By copying and pasting the address into a search engine, Luis found more information about the home on a website called realestatesales.biz. Notably, the house was last purchased in 1980 and went into something called foreclosure in 1989. Luis did not know what foreclosure meant.

There was a link at the bottom of the page that read *Public Record*. Luis clicked on it, and a spreadsheet with a long list of names appeared on the screen. Confused, he scrolled down. The names were listed alphabetically. Luis came to the *R* section and found the name *Rollins*.

The appearance of the name on the screen made him shiver. The name beside Rollins was Stacy. Maybe that was Timothy's mom. Giving it more consideration, Luis thought it may not be a big deal for the name Rollins to appear on the list. There were hundreds of other R names on the list.

Then he saw it. Next to the name was an address. 1669 Croydon St., Philadelphia. Beside the address in red letters was the word *Foreclosure*. At that moment his phone buzzed, startling him. He threw it across the room in a panic.

Immediately he realized his mistake. The buzz was a text alert, not a spirit from the great beyond. He walked over to the phone and picked it up. He was relieved to see the glass undamaged. There was a text from Rian.

RIAN
whatsup?????

The message read. He immediately replied.

LUIS
nothing

RIAN
i got my phone back! 😄

LUIS

RIAN
r u ready for tmrw?

LUIS
idk

RIAN
dont get scared. we got this!!!

LUIS
we have problem

RIAN
problem?

LUIS
im investigating

RIAN
investigating what?

LUIS
1669 croydon st.

RIAN
????

LUIS
shacks house

RIAN
you want to throw eggs at it?

LUIS
no. the house!!!

RIAN
oooooooooooook

LUIS
i found it. www.realestatesales.biz
it was TR house!

RIAN
really??? cool!

LUIS
not cool. he haunt me today!

RIAN

LUIS
true
he haunt me in the bathroom

RIAN
in the br? r u ok? 😥

LUIS
no joke. this is dangerous

RIAN
u r just nervous about tmrw
we will not be pushed around

LUIS
I thinkk something bad will happen

RIAN
wheels are in motion
no turning back now

The glimmer from Julio's gold crucifix shimmered around his neck. Luis looked up and saw his father standing in the doorway, his arms braced to either side of the jam. Julio touched his wrist as if pointing to a watch.

Time-to go to sleep, he signed.

Luis held up his index finger to ask his father for *one more minute* and returned to his phone.

LUIS
bedtime.
gtg

RIAN
big day tmrw!
get some sleep. gn 💤

He lowered the phone and placed it on the nightstand beside his bed. Julio tucked his son tightly in under the sheets and shut off the light.

Luis didn't sleep well that night. He kept thinking about Timothy Rollins, and the house and what happened in the bathroom. When he did finally fall asleep, he had a nightmare.

In the dream, he was locked inside the kiln with the art teacher, Mrs. Miller. She was screaming at Luis without making a sound. He had no idea what she was saying, but from the way her face contorted as she spoke, she appeared furious and terrified.

She grabbed the tiles piled on shelves inside the kiln and smashed them one at a time onto the floor. After smashing enough tiles to create a knee-high mound of crushed clay, she came to Luis's tile. A black tile with Superman's trademark *S* carved into the center.

She didn't smash Luis's tile. She inspected it carefully turning it over as if she were looking for something. Then without warning, she put it in her mouth and started eating it. Her jaw gnashed the ceramic tiles unnaturally. As she pushed it further into her mouth, her teeth began to break as she took large, exaggerated bites. Ceramic and enamel broke apart and fell all around her.

Clay dust fell from the corners of her upturned smile. The more her jaw gnashed the tile, the more clay dust fell around her. Eventually she was buried beneath a pile of orange dust and tile fragments. He could not see her anymore.

Carefully, Luis reached out to touch the heaping mound encasing his teacher. Without warning, a hand burst from it and grabbed him. He tried to pull away, but the hand was like a vice grip around his wrist. As he pulled back, a figure emerged from the pile of dust. The figure that emerged was Shack.

Luis was awoken by his mother. He had managed a paltry three hours of sleep and woke up in a cold sweat. Frightened about the day's prospects and exhausted from lack of sleep, Luis readied himself for school.

30

LIPSTICK

Rian and Hassan stood outside the boys' bathroom. They had a small window of time to plant the glasses before Shack got there.

Language Arts started every day at 8:21. By 8:23 Shack would ask to go to the bathroom. These two events were as regular as clockwork. Rian picked up on the daily routine sometime in early October and wondered how Mrs. Bae-Huley failed to notice.

Eventually it occurred to Rian that Mrs. Bae-Huley was perfectly aware and almost certainly preferred to have him out of the room, even if only for ten minutes.

Rian and Hassan started their morning in Hearing Support with Miss Hughes, trying to determine whether words ended in *d, b,* or *t.*

At 8:16 they aroused no suspicion when they asked Miss Hughes to send them back to Mrs. Bae-Huley's class a few minutes earlier than usual. Instead of heading to the classroom however, they went straight for the second-floor boys' bathroom.

Rian checked her watch. It read 8:18. She made sure to set it to Mrs. Bae-Huley's clock the day before. She did not want to overestimate the amount of time they had to execute the plan.

"Are you going in?" Rian asked Hassan. "We only have three minutes."

"OK. Give it to me," said Hassan.

Rian dug into the front pocket of her backpack without looking and pulled her hand out abruptly.

"Ouch," she said. "Something burned me."

Hassan looked at her confused and reached into the bag. He pulled out the angular rimmed glasses Rian found in Shack's oven. They hoped the old spectacles might be good enough to pass for Timothy Rollin's glasses. Hassan noticed that they did feel warm.

He wiggled his fingers across his face and signed, *Weird*.

"Hurry," Rian urged him.

Without further hesitation Hassan slipped into the bathroom and saw Luis standing in the center of the room with his arms folded.

"Lou? Why you here?" Hassan asked.

You-need to-stop, Luis signed. *T-R is-real! Give me-the glasses!*

Real? Hassan asked his friend, confused.

Ghost! Luis signed with wide eyes and his index fingers pinched to his thumbs.

Outside the bathroom, Rian was getting more nervous with each passing moment. The time was 8:22, and Shack was due for his morning constitutional at any moment.

She opened the bathroom door and called out, "Hassan, what are you doing? We need to go!"

Hassan hurried over to the door and told her of Luis's protest. She looked down the hall and saw it was clear. Then she entered the bathroom.

"What are you doing?" she asked Luis. "We have to hurry."

We-have to-change-the plan. This-isn't-safe. Luis responded turning his fists outward as if he were breaking shackles from his wrist.

Hassan turned to Rian and shrugged. Clutched in his right hand was a tube of red lipstick. The cap was removed.

211

"Give it to me," she said.

Hassan looked back at Luis. Luis shook his head no. He looked at Rian, and she held out her hand.

"If you don't want to do it, fine, but don't stop me!" she said, her hand still outstretched.

Hassan handed the lipstick over to Rian with a nod. She immediately got to work writing on the mirror. In large red letters Rian wrote the message, 'Give It All Back!' She stepped back to study her handiwork and felt a lump in her throat. It didn't look like a message from beyond the grave. It looked like the work of a sixth-grade girl. It looked like her handwriting.

She turned to Hassan. "Give them to me."

He reached into his pocket and removed the angular gold-rimmed glasses. She took them and turned to place them in the sink. Suddenly, the creek of an overhead hinge stopped her in her tracks. The bathroom door opened and Shack entered the room.

He stopped in his tracks when he saw the three of them together. His eyes went directly to Rian, and his face turned red.

"What is she doing in here?" Shack cried. "This is the boys' room."

Rian couldn't speak. She stood staring at Shack with her mouth agape. Luis and Hassan were no help. They froze in place. They weren't prepared for this situation either. It was Hassan who finally spoke.

"We tell you this a boys' room," he said, turning to Rian.

Rian still said nothing. She wasn't looking at Hassan. She was watching Shack's eyes move from her to the mirror directly behind them and the red words written in her handwriting across the mirror glass. 'Give It All Back!'

After reading the message Shack's eyes returned to Rian. His glare made her flinch, and she dropped the glasses from her hand. The gold angular glasses hit the ceramic tile hard.

"You? You three? You're T-R? How did you know about…" Shack's expression shifted from confusion to anger.

"You're dead," he said in a sickeningly calm, low manner.

He grabbed Hassan's collar and pulled him close. Hassan, having never been in a fight in his life, closed his eyes and prepared to be hit. Before Shack could reach back however, the bathroom door opened once again.

Quickly, Shack released Hassan, and they all turned to the door. A voice singing out loud, preceded a face. "A boy stood on the railroad tracks, and didn't hear the bell…" the performance stopped abruptly.

It was Mr. Herman. He sized them up. An unread copy of the *Philadelphia Inquirer* rested under his right arm, and a twelve-ounce mug of freshly brewed coffee was held tightly in his left hand. He looked at them with one eyebrow raised.

"What are you children doing here? Rain, this is a boy's bathroom," he said in a manner that suggested she was unaware of that fact.

Rian stood before Shack, Mr. Herman, and her friends, mortified. The situation was beyond bad. It was off the rails, down a ravine, into the river, and over the falls bad.

She was caught. Not just caught by Shack and Mr. Herman, caught by herself. She had convinced herself she had the strength to get back at Shack. Not the physical strength but she had the mental strength. The personal fortitude to not back down and to have her revenge. To have her day. Apparently, she was wrong.

"Rain? Rain? Are you going to answer me, Rain?" Mr. Herman insisted.

"Rian!" she yelled at the top of her lungs. "My name is Rian!"

It just came out. Perhaps it was the sense of hopelessness that the situation presented. Maybe the city had turned her into a miscreant after all. Whatever the reason, that was the moment Rian had enough and finally corrected Mr. Herman's mistake.

"Rian? You mean, your name's not Rain?" he asked dumbfounded. "I'm sorry. Why didn't you tell me sooner?"

213

Rian shrugged. This was not the reaction she expected. "I just. I tried. I don't know," she trailed off.

"That still doesn't answer my question. What are you doing here, Rian?" As he spoke, his eyes went to the writing on the mirror.

"What is that? Defacing school property?" he asked.

"It's just lipstick," Rian held out the lipstick as she spoke. She immediately looked at Shack who watched her like a hawk.

"Ugh. What am I supposed to do about that?" Mr. Herman asked, pointing to the mirror. He looked at his watch and rolled his eyes.

"Look, I have thirty minutes before my class comes back from Gym. If I report this I will need Mr. Rose, and I'll need the principal. I don't need any of that. Not on my prep. Who wrote it on the wall?" asked Mr. Herman.

Rian sheepishly raised her hand. Shack's eyes remained locked on her.

"You can't stay, and clean it up. Luis." He pointed at Luis and then turned to Hassan.

"Tell him to clean up the lipstick." As he spoke to Hassan, Mr. Herman's hands waved back and forth as if cleaning an imaginary mirror.

Luis flicked his index finger up near his right temple.

"He understand," Hassan said directly back to Mr. Herman.

"The rest of you get out of here. You're supposed to be in Art. You're late."

Shack left first. Hassan and Rian looked at each other and quickly followed. Luis stayed back and wiped red lipstick off the mirror.

31

REVENGE

Shack entered the Art room first. Students were sitting four to a table, gluing strips of muslin fabric to plastic bottle sculptures. Wayne was working at a table in the back of the room, near the kiln. His eyes went immediately to Shack. Shack's eyes went immediately to Wayne.

"Mr. Shack, you're ten minutes late," said Mrs. Miller dryly.

"I was in the bathroom," Shack answered without looking at her or breaking stride.

"Get your bottle, and get started," said Mrs. Miller.

With his backpack slung over his left shoulder, Shack walked to the back of the classroom to retrieve a plastic water bottle with sculpture wire and clothespins sticking out of the top.

The table was close to the kiln. Shack could feel Wayne's eyes locked on him. Wayne almost certainly knew what was in his backpack. The useless little treasures belonging to his classmates filled the bag beyond capacity.

Shack grabbed his project and sat at the empty table across from Wayne. An unusual choice since there was an empty seat two tables up beside Ben Ellis.

As he sat on the stool he marveled at how close he had come to being fooled by the deaf kids. He had really believed he was haunted and that he needed to return the stolen items to his classmates or else. Or else what?

What were they going to do if he hadn't returned the items? And why did they want him to put everything in the kiln?

He turned and gave Wayne a sideways glance. Wayne's head pivoted from Shack back to his sculpture.

Just then, Rian and Hassan entered the classroom.

Mrs. Miller turned to them exasperated and asked, "Where were the two of you?"

"We were in the bathroom," exclaimed Rian.

"You too? Was there an issue with breakfast?" she asked.

Rian scanned the room, searching for Shack. She saw him at the back table near the kiln, next to Wayne. She needed to warn Wayne to abandon the plan.

Rian and Hassan walked to the back of the room and retrieved their projects. Shack never took his eyes off of them. He wanted to make sure they didn't sign to Wayne. He was curious to see this plan play out. He knew it was no coincidence that Wayne was sitting next to the kiln, and he wasn't about to let him off the hook.

Rian and Hassan grabbed their bottles and sat at Sandra's table. They were far from Wayne, far from Shack, and far from the kiln.

For thirty long minutes they worked on their sculptures, waiting for someone to make a move. Even after Luis entered, they did nothing. As the period came to a close Mrs. Miller told the students to line up and wait for Mrs. Bae-Huley. She stood outside the door at the front of the line. It was her routine to engage Mrs. Bae-Huley in a short conversation outside the room as they handed off the class like a baton, from one to the other.

Shack recognized his opportunity. He lingered at his table while the others lined up. He picked up his bag and headed over to the kiln. The kiln's door was open just a bit. He slid his backpack off his shoulder and dropped it to the floor.

Wayne also lingered. Shack pretended not to notice. He turned to make sure no one else was looking, and he slowly opened the kiln door. He crouched down and unzipped his bag, dug around a bit and pulled out a compact mirror that he stole from Elisha. He opened it and held the mirrored top in a way that allowed him to see behind his back.

Wayne was coming up behind him. Now he knew the plan. They were going to push him into the kiln. It was brilliant.

Too bad, Shack thought to himself. *This just isn't their day.*

Wayne approached carefully. Shack was squatting, which would make it easy for Wayne to push him forward. Now inches away, Wayne put both hands on Shack's shoulders and heaved.

Shack was ready for Wayne. He grabbed his wrist and swung him around, tossing *him* into the kiln. With the class filtering out of the room, Shack grabbed the door and swung it shut, sealing Wayne inside. He scooped up the compact, shoved it back into his bag, and hurried to the back of the line.

Shack confidently strode to meet the others, never taking his eyes off of them. Rian looked at Luis, who looked at Sandra, who looked at Hassan. The line filtered out of the room, but all five of them stayed back.

"Don't even think about letting him out," Shack warned them.

"Stop us!" Sandra demanded, passing Shack as she marched toward the kiln.

He got ahead of her and placed his big body between them and the door to the kiln. Sandra tried to move him, but it was useless. She might as well try to carry away the kiln instead. Shack was immovable.

You-want me to-beat you up-again? Luis signed.

"You thought you were gonna fool me? That's funny. You can't fool me. I'm going to make every last one of you pay. I don't care if you are deaf or crippled. You're all dead!" Shack threatened.

A small rattling sound came from inside the kiln. Shack heard it right away, as did Sandra. They figured it was probably just Wayne trying to get out, but steadily the rattle got louder. Before long, it escalated in intensity and became a banging sound. The banging got louder and louder. There was no way Wayne could make the noise. The kiln was shaking now, and Shack stepped away from it, confused.

"What did you do?" Rian said to Shack as Luis pulled on the handle to open the kiln.

"I did exactly what you were going to do to me!" Shack replied.

Shack pushed Luis and grabbed the handle. He pulled with all of his might, but the door was stuck.

"Look!" Hassan cried, pointing to the temperature gauge.

The thermometer was increasing in temperature.

"He's gonna die in there!" Sandra shouted.

"This is your fault, not mine! You were going to push me in. You were all going to push me in!" Shack was shouting, the panic in his voice was clear.

Luis once again grabbed the handle and pulled, but it was no use. Hassan furiously pressed buttons to stop the machine, but nothing worked. The temperature continued to rise.

"Help! Help, Wayne is stuck in the kiln!" Rian called out.

The intensity of the rattling and banging of the big blue behemoth had already captured Mrs. Miller's attention. She charged back into the room. Mrs. Bae-Huley and the rest of the class followed.

"What are you children doing? You're not allowed to touch that. No one is allowed to touch that except me!" Mrs. Miller had to yell in order to compensate for the incredible noise filling the room.

Shack was now pulling on the door with Luis trying to open it. The thermometer read 500 degrees.

"You can't open it!" Mrs. Miller shouted.

"Turn it off. We have to get him out!" yelled Rian at Mrs. Miller.

"What are you talking about?" she yelled back.

"Wayne. He's stuck! Inside!" Sandra screamed.

"What?" Mrs. Miller shrieked.

She immediately started pushing buttons trying to turn it off. It didn't work. The temperature continued to climb. Seven hundred degrees, eight hundred, nine hundred. As the temperature inside the kiln climbed so too did the temperature in the Art room. The whole class was now back inside watching the scene unfold. Everyone was sweating as heat radiated all around them.

"I can't shut it off. What have you done?" she asked looking at Shack.

They stared helplessly as the kiln reached its top temperature, one thousand eight hundred degrees. Rian, Hassan, Sandra, and Luis sobbed. There was no way their friend could survive. They were responsible. Shack may have pushed him in, but their actions allowed it to happen.

The kiln banged so loudly it made the building shake. Tremors made the Art room reverberate all around them.

"We have to get out of here!" Mrs. Miller yelled to the class as she turned away from the kiln. "There is something wrong with it. We are all in danger."

There was one last loud bang, an explosive burst of sound like a bomb had gone off. For a moment, everyone in the room was deaf, their ears ringing with pain. The classroom door swung shut. Mrs. Bae-Huley grabbed the handle, and it burned her hand.

"We're trapped. God help us!" she cried.

The class huddled together as far away from the kiln as they could stand. The banging had stopped. The room was no longer shaking, and the temperature inside the kiln dropped precipitously. Then, the lights went out.

The Art room remained hot. The thermostat read 101 degrees. The sound of crying filled the room. No one could believe what they were witnessing. Their classmate, Wayne, was surely dead. Burned alive inside Mrs. Miller's kiln of death.

Suddenly, the kiln door swung open, and smoke billowed out into the room. Sobs turned to coughs as the smoke choked the students. Rian stared at the kiln, certain she saw something moving inside. A figure emerged from the tomb.

"Wayne?" she thought to herself. "How is it possible?"

As the smoke started to clear everyone saw a figure coming out of the kiln. It was walking toward them.

"Oh, thank god! Wayne, you're alive!" Mrs. Miller ran to him. "Someone call 9-1-1."

She was within arm's length of the figure when the lights came back on. Mrs. Miller froze in terror. She could not believe what she saw standing in front of her. The person who came out of the kiln was not the person who entered. It was a ghost. A ghost from her past. A ghost she had tried to forget for more than thirty years. Standing in front of her was Timothy Rollins.

He was small, not much taller than Mrs. Miller. His straight blonde hair, once shiny and neat, had lost its luster from decades of death. His pale white face was covered in a layer of ash, and his eyes were black coals. His braces remained on his rotted teeth, and his clothes, relics of the 1980s, were tattered and burned.

"Where are they?" Timothy's words choked out of his throat.

"Timothy? It can't be! It can't be!" Mrs. Miller stared at the boy with her eyes white and wide. Her mouth hung open, and her body trembled with fear.

Luis turned to Rian and thrust his index finger from his chin to her face, repeating the same sign again and again.

I told you! I told you! Luis signed indignantly.

Rian couldn't believe her eyes. She wanted to run, but her feet were cemented to the floor. Every one of Mrs. Bae-Huley's students watched the scene unfolding before them, wondering what it was they were witnessing.

"Where are they?" Timothy repeated the question and stepped closer to Mrs. Miller, his voice deep and threatening, mismatched to the diminutive shape standing before her.

"No. Timothy. You're dead. It can't be!" Mrs. Miller backed away from him as she spoke, tripping over a chair and landing on her back.

He stood over her and said, "Hello, Mrs. Miller. Do you have my glasses?"

"I'm sorry. I didn't mean to do it. I didn't know. I swear to god, I had no idea!"

Mrs. Miller turned herself over and scrambled to her feet but fell back down, clumsily. She tried to get to the door, but she couldn't get to her feet. Furiously she crawled away from him.

"Help me!" she screamed. "He's come back. He's come back for me! I'm sorry, Timothy. I'm sorry!"

Mrs. Miller finally got to her feet and pushed her way through the children. She reached out and grabbed the door handle. She clasped it tight and felt her hand sizzle from the extreme heat still radiating from it. She was so scared she failed to notice the burn at all. She turned the handle and opened the door.

"Help!" she screamed as she ran down the empty hallway and disappeared around the corner.

The other students in the building were sheltered in place in their classrooms. Mr. Tasker had interpreted the shaking as an earthquake and called for emergency procedures.

Jamilah Massulah and Reg Mosely turned and headed for the door, but it slammed shut in front of them. The handle now glowed bright red, daring someone to pull it open.

"Where are they? Where are my glasses?" as the volume in Timothy's voice increased in intensity, the temperature in the room once again began to rise.

One by one, the ceramic tiles laid out neatly in the front of the class rose off the black table surface and levitated in place. Then, as if fired from a slingshot, the tiles whizzed about the room, smashing into walls, shattering collections of student art and breaking the tall vertical window panes behind Mrs. Miller's desk.

Shack looked at a now-glassless windowpane and considered running through it. The Art room was on the second floor, but it was positioned at the front of the building, not the back. A jump from the window would not be as far a fall down, and if he were lucky he might land in a bush below.

"Forget this," he said, making a run for the window.

His long clumsy stride drew Timothy's attention.

"Lombardo!" Timothy yelled the name in a piercing cry that caused everyone to cover their ears. Everyone but Luis.

Suddenly, Shack wasn't running forward any longer. He was running up. Just like the tiles he now was levitating off the ground.

"Lombardo! Where are my glasses?" Timothy screamed at Shack.

"I'm not Lombardo. Put me down. Please, put me down. I don't want to die!" Shack cried out and choked back tears as his limbs continued to convulse in the air, helplessly looking for the ground.

He tried to propel himself toward the window but just flailed as he hung suspended in the air.

"I don't want to die," Shack wailed. The sight of him crying out in fear, even in that moment of chaos, was not lost on his classmates.

Then the large double-bowl stainless steel sink exploded like a geyser, gushing water with such force it hit the ceiling and ricocheted back down onto the students below.

It's our-fault, Luis signed, pushing his fingertips into his shoulder and dropping his arm to his side.

Rian knew what to do. The glasses she found in the oven at the house. The glasses she tried to use to stage a prank on Shack. They were Timothy Rollins's glasses.

Glasses, she signed to Luis, bringing her hands to her eyes.

Luis looked at her, confused.

Bathroom! Rian signed furiously.

Luis understood. The glasses they tried to plant in the bathroom. When Rian and Hassan left, he saw them on the floor.

Trash, he signed with his palm to his forehead.

The students were huddled together away from Timothy and Shack. The heat continued to climb in the room, and they shielded themselves from the scalding hot spray, still gushing from the sink. It was hard to distinguish their sweat from the water.

Now Luis had an idea. He ran to the back of the room, away from the group and toward the kiln. In a drawer under Mrs. Miller's work station were a pair of cowhide welding gloves. He remembered her showing them to the class the day she started firing the tiles.

He grabbed the gloves and ran to Rian.

Leave, Luis signed and pointed to the door.

Luis slid the gloves over his hands as they broke away from the other kids and ran to the door.

Timothy Rollins was standing nose to nose with Shack, who hung upside, suspended in midair.

"Give them back," he growled in Shack's face.

The smell of burned flesh oozed from his mouth and hit Shack's nostrils, causing him to gag. He sobbed the same three words over and over again as he hung in front of this deathly thing.

"I'm not Lombardo," he wailed incoherently.

With the gloves over his hands, Luis stared at the bright red door handle. He was unsure just how well the gloves would protect him. He took a breath, closed his eyes, and shot his hand out, grabbing the handle. He twisted it with all of his might, and the door opened.

Rian and Luis ran out of the room, tearing Timothy's attention away from Shack and placing it squarely on them. They ran down the hall toward the bathroom. Every time they passed a door a furious explosion of water erupted from a classroom sink, sending the faucet skyward. Steam filled the hallways and the classrooms as the building started to shake once again.

Timothy's voice rumbled from behind them. They were running in a tunnel, trying to escape an oncoming train.

"Give me my glasses!" the voice boomed all around them. The vibrations caused by his speech made the walls shake.

Student artwork and hallway bulletin boards spontaneously combusted, sending flames shooting out from the walls. The fire licked their cheeks and singed their hair. They kept moving, however, as if their lives depended on it.

At last they arrived at the bathroom. They burst through the door and found a foot of water on the floor. The flood had caused the garbage can to tip over and its contents floated in the hot water.

They scanned the room, but in their panic they couldn't see the glasses. The water temperature started to rise even higher. Unable to take the heat, Luis climbed up on the sink and dangled his legs over the side. Rian pressed on.

Reaching her hand down, she swiped back and forth hoping to touch something recognizable. There they were. She could feel the bent rims and thick glass. Plunging her hand further down, Rian grasped for the glasses. With one swipe, she clutched them in her hand.

"I got them!" she yelled, holding them up to Luis.

Give them to him? Luis asked with a puzzled expression.

"You got a better idea?" Rian asked.

Luis jumped back into the water, and they ran out of the bathroom back toward the Art room. The hallways were filled with scalding hot water as the students' screams rang out of classrooms. Some sloshed around, looking for escape while others climbed onto their desks to avoid the hot water.

The sound of Timothy's voice seemed to come from all directions, though he was nowhere to be seen.

"We have them!" Rian stopped running and stood her ground. She thrust the glasses into the air and continued her call. "Timothy Rollins, we have your glasses. I have your glasses."

They found Timothy walking down the middle of the hallway toward them. Undaunted, Rian held the glasses in front of her body and walked toward Timothy Rollins. They met just outside of Mrs. Miller's Art room.

"Here. I believe these belong to you," Rian said, her statement sounded like a question as she held out the glasses and waited.

He inspected them carefully. They seemed a perfect fit for this undead boy standing before her. He reached out and took them from her. After careful examination he placed the glasses on his face and smiled.

"Thank you," he said to her graciously.

"I'm sorry for what happened to you," Rian said, rolling her fist around her chest.

Timothy placed his balled-up fist, or what was left of it, in the center of his chest and copied her sign.

Then without warning, he abruptly turned around and walked past the class who were all standing and watching the scene unfold. He disappeared back into the Art room. The temperature of the receding water decreased, the walls stopped shaking, and the bulletin boards around them were bare, with nothing left to burn. The hallway was silent.

And then a crash came from inside the Art room. The students, led by Rian and Luis charged into the room to see what happened. They found

Shack face down on the floor. He was crying and clutching his knees to his chest. As he sobbed, he repeated the same four words over and over again to himself, "Please don't hurt me. Please don't hurt me".

Timothy Rollins was standing in front of the kiln. Rian, Luis, Hassan, Sandra and the rest of Mrs. Bae-Huley's class watched him intently to see what he would do.

He stared back at them. He lifted his boney right hand and waved at Rian and Luis. They waved back, unsure how to interpret what was happening. Then he grabbed the door and swung it shut, sealing himself inside. The loud bang echoed throughout the room. It echoed in the student's ears. It echoed in Rian's implants, and it echoed in Luis's body. Just as suddenly as he had arrived, Timothy Rollins was gone.

Wayne! Luis signed, running back to the kiln.

When he got to the kiln he tapped lightly on the handle to make sure it wasn't hot. When he saw that it wasn't, he pulled the handle, and the door swung open.

Smoke billowed out of the machine. Momentarily filling the room, making it impossible for anyone to see any further than a few feet in front of them. The students coughed and waved their hands to push the smoke away from their faces. A few moments later, smoke disappeared on its own.

As it cleared, a figure could be seen inside the kiln. Clearing his eyes and straining to look, Luis saw a familiar face. Standing inside the kiln was Wayne. He was confused and disoriented.

"What happened?" he asked flipping his index fingers toward the floor.

Luis ran to his friend and threw his arms around Wayne. Rian, Hassan, and Sandra ran over and joined in the embrace. They stood there for a long time holding each other. Wayne was safe. They were all safe.

Meanwhile, Ben walked over to Shack who remained balled up on the floor, still talking to himself.

"You okay?" he asked.

Ben's voice got Shack's attention. For a moment, he stopped sobbing and looked up at his friend. Shack got to his feet and wiped his tear stained cheeks. The class was now looking at him and his backpack, which was open and laying on the floor beside his feet. Their belongings had fallen out and were sprawled out all around him.

"What are you looking at?" he yelled at the group.

Lucas broke away from the others and walked up to Shack. He was standing toe to toe with this bully who had tormented him for years.

"What?" Shack asked, his voice cracked, and his lip trembled.

Lucas reached down and picked up his Rubik's Cube.

"I'll just take this," he said, retrieving his toy, turning his back and walking away from Shack.

The other students followed Lucas's lead, one by one they stared Shack down and reclaimed their belongings from him. Within minutes, everything was back with its' rightful owners.

Still holding each other, they didn't notice that Antoine Kennedy had started to clap. They didn't immediately notice when the other students joined him. Before long, everyone was applauding and cheering. Rian poked her head up from the group hug and watched. She nudged Sandra, then Luis, then Hassan and Wayne. As they turned to their classmates, the celebration grew louder and more boisterous.

They had saved the school and ended Shack's reign of terror. Wayne was safe and John Hancock had not burned to the ground.

They were heroes. It was finally their day.

EPILOGUE

It took time for life to return to normal at Hancock, but eventually it did. Timothy Rollins disappeared as abruptly as he had arrived. No one was seriously hurt, the damage to the school was minimal, and in time, the events of that day became nothing more than Millbrook Park folklore.

Rian, Luis, Hassan, Sandra and Wayne enjoyed new-found popularity after the smoke cleared, and the water receded. There was a sudden interest among their classmates in learning sign language. Rian and Hassan spent many lunches teaching Elisha, Jenna, Jamilah, Reg Mosley, and even Nathan Powers sign language. By the end of the year the misfit table had become the must-sit table.

Mrs. Miller disappeared after Timothy's resurgence. It was reported that she finally decided to retire, but no one at Hancock ever saw her again. She did not come back at the end of the year to complete her last tile installation. A new Art teacher, Mr. Milligan, took over, cementing and grouting the four by four squares to a little piece of real estate next to the nurse's office.

Mr. Herman hung in for a few more years. He managed to stick around longer than Mrs. Bae-Huley, who retired the following year. Mrs. Hughes and Mr. Rose remained beloved fixtures at Hancock for decades, working with other deaf and hard of hearing children.

Before the end of the summer, Joanna found a job close to Penn Hills. She and Rian packed their belongings and moved out of Millbrook Park in early August. Rian continued to keep in touch with Luis and Sandra by text and even came down to the city to visit them a couple of times in seventh and eighth grade.

Luis finally got his wish to attend the Pennsylvania School for the Deaf and was a star on the seventh-grade intramural basketball team. Hassan and Wayne remained together throughout their middle school years while Sandra returned to her neighborhood school, Woodrow Wilson Middle School. She and Luis still text often.

Despite the distance and the continued movement in their lives, they all remained friends. Never before and never again would Rian find a group of people quite like the friends she made at John Hancock Elementary School in Millbrook Park, Philadelphia.

ABOUT THE AUTHOR

Christian Fusco, author of *deaf not Deaf*,

is a twenty year veteran teacher of the Deaf and Hard of Hearing who's worked in and around Philadelphia throughout his career. He studied education at Indiana University of Pennsylvania and Film and Media Arts at Temple University. He's taught filmmaking at the Bryn Mawr Film Institute for the past ten years. After receiving his graduate degree in Educational Administration from Scranton University in 2017 he was elected to his local school board where he currently serves as vice-president. He is a father and a husband who loves traveling with his family above all else.

Made in the USA
Las Vegas, NV
13 July 2021